HIGH
COUNTRY

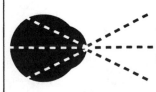

This Large Print Book carries the
Seal of Approval of N.A.V.H.

HIGH COUNTRY

PETER DAWSON

Thorndike Press • Thorndike, Maine

Library of Congress Cataloging in Publication Data:

Dawson, Peter, 1907–
    High country / by Peter Dawson.
       p.   cm.
    ISBN 1-56054-523-2 (alk. paper : lg. print)
    1. Large type books.   I. Title.
    [PS3507.A848H5   1992]   92-25384
    813'.54—dc20   CIP

Thorndike Large Print® Western Series edition published
in 1992 by arrangement with the Golden West Literary
Agency.

Cover photo by Thayer Smith.

The tree indicium is a trademark of Thorndike Press.

This book is printed on acid-free, high opacity paper. ∞

HIGH
COUNTRY

I

He knew now where he had made his mistake. He had turned up this canyon late yesterday, and they had let him come. He was seeing the reason as he looked up through the crests of the pines to the sheer two-hundred-foot rise of granite at this dead end of the box.

He could hear one of them moving through the brush up there along the rim. Only an hour ago he had caught a glimpse of the second, leisurely following him. So now he rode back to the margin of the trees, wound the reins around the horn, swung wearily aground and slapped the steeldust across the rump, watching the animal trot out into the open. Then he called:

"Hold it. I'm coming out."

He unbuckled the shell-belt and, with it hanging from his left hand, followed the horse.

The muscles along his wide back tightened in fear until shortly a voice called down from the rim, "Drop it and keep goin'," and he did, a dozen paces. Then he sat down and rested his arms across his knees and laid his head against them. He had never been so tired.

He heard the man up there whistle shrilly and it was maybe three minutes before a slow hoof-thud sounded close by and he lifted his head to see the lanky rider on the sorrel coming toward him from the trees down-canyon. He watched while this one rode over to the steeldust and caught the reins. Then he was no longer interested and dropped his head again, drowsily listening as the man rode around him and stopped, probably to pick up his Colt's.

Jim Sherill must have dozed then, for later he came violently awake at something jarring his shoulder. Looking up, he saw the second man close beside him, thrusting boot back into stirrup after nudging him.

This one, stocky and barrel-bodied and with a face darkened by a black stubble of beard, said, "Time to move."

Jim Sherill got up and trudged stiffly across to the steeldust, a tall and big-boned man whose wide shoulders sagged in exhaustion. He wondered if they'd think it strange he didn't ask where they were taking him, decided finally they wouldn't.

They spent the better part of an hour working out of the dry bed of the canyon, finally climbing a deer-trail he hadn't spotted on his way up. Two hours later at dusk, and ten miles lower in the heavily-timbered and canyon-shot foothills, they rode down across a long grassy meadow toward a light winking out of a stand of jackpine.

Jim Sherill had slept through most of this long interval and now, as they came to a creek winding through the meadow, he pulled in and climbed from the saddle and knelt at the stream's edge, laying wide hat aside as the steeldust eagerly nosed the water. He cupped his hands and drank as fast as he could swallow and, his day-long thirst finally slaked, threw water over his blond head and scrubbed his face.

The thickset rider drawled, "Brother, you must've needed that," as he climbed back into leather.

Sherill gave the speaker an impassive look, his deep brown eyes humorless, and they went on. He was feeling better now, refreshed even more by the sleep than by the drink, and he took some pains to look carefully about him in the fading light as they rode in on the light. What held his eye longest was a big half-acre pole corral holding maybe fifty head of horses and, abreast it, the dying coals of a fire. The rest — a smaller corral closer in, the sheds, the sideless hay barn, the big bunkhouse and smaller cabin beyond

— was the usual for a hill ranch.

The five men loafing at the bunkhouse door paid them a strict and silent attention as they approached. The stocky one called, "Boss in?" and the nearest man tilted his head toward the small cabin beyond, saying, "Yeah," his eye upon Sherill as he asked, "Where'd you pick him up?"

He got no answer and shortly they came aground and racked their horses at a tie-rail in the trees directly below the cabin. Then Jim Sherill was following the stocky rider through the cabin's door and into a room crammed with the necessary odds and ends to running a ranch.

There was a desk littered with ledgers and tally book and several copies of the *Stockmen's Gazette*. Two saddles were rope-hung from roof joists, and there were bridles, ropes and a disorderly heap of saddle-blankets and bear-skin chaps in a back corner. A rack above the desk held three carbines and a shotgun. There was a swivel-chair and two other battered chairs held together by baling wire. There was a man.

This man standing behind the flat-topped desk facing the door was perhaps a couple of inches shorter than Sherill, which put him close to six feet. He was thin almost to gauntness. His hair was salt-and-pepper and his eyes were of the palest gray, icy. Across his flat open-vested middle ran a heavy gold chain with a bear's-claw pendant hanging from it. He wore a Colt's butt-foremost and high at his left side. The eyes and his long-fingered hands tied in with the weapon in Sherill's inspection of him. He was perhaps forty but looked older.

He said, "You're a day late, Lockwood," his glance incuriously touching Jim Sherill and then settling on the stocky man. In speaking, his lips barely moved.

"Here's our reason." Lockwood jerked a thumb at Sherill.

Now those pale eyes settled full on Sherill and the boss drawled, "Well?"

"We cut his sign four days ago," Lockwood told him. "Up at the border shack. That blue was missin' from the corral and a bay branded VR had been left in his place. Me and Slim got to wonderin' why and followed the blue's sign. We'd finished what you sent us up for."

"Got the money, Mitch?"

Mitch Lockwood drew a leather pouch from inside his shirt and laid it on the desk, and the other said, "Go ahead."

"Well, we finally caught up with this jasper late last night. He got away and took a wrong swing up Six Mile Canyon. We played with

11

him the rest of last night and today, took turns keepin' him on the move. Two hours ago he wound up in the box. So we brought him on in. That's all of it, Ed."

The boss reached down to the desk and picked up the shredded stub of a cigar, musing, "VR." He lit the cigar. "Regina Victoria, eh?" He eyed Jim Sherill through the billowing fog of smoke. "The Queen's brand. So you're a Mounty."

"No," Sherill said.

Ed eased his angular frame down into the swivel-chair and cocked his boots on the desk's scarred edge, saying with scarcely a movement of the lips, "We got all night for this. How come the VR?"

"Had to leave a certain place in a hurry."

"In Canada?"

Sherill nodded.

Slim, the lanky one, now stepped over and laid Sherill's holstered gun and belt on the desk, saying, "It's a Colt's, Ed. If he's a Mounty, he didn't swipe the Queen's hardware."

Ed moved his dark head from side to side. "He wouldn't if he was smart. And if he was smart he wouldn't ride a royal-branded horse into this country. Which he didn't." He looked up at Sherill, said, "Talk, stranger."

12

"Suppose I did steal your horse?" Sherill asked.

Mitch Lockwood chuckled softly and with enough meaning to draw a thin smile from the older man, who drawled, "Suppose you did. And you stole the first one, too? The one with the VR?"

"Yes."

"Prove it."

"I can't."

"Where were you headed?"

"Across the Missouri and up to Whitewater. Further maybe."

"Then why'd you pick this way to come? Fifty miles west you could've made it easy. The same goes for over east. Instead, you head into country even the Sioux used to keep shy of."

"Figured they wouldn't bother to follow. Or, if they did, that I could lose 'em."

Ed narrowed an eye against the cigar's curl of smoke. His glance held coldly to Sherill for perhaps a quarter-minute.

At length he drawled, "You didn't steal that VR jughead. You're with the police and you're no deserter. If you were runnin', you'd pick an easy way across the line. Which you didn't. You were sent down here. This is the place you were headed. How do I know? Because this is the only big outfit in the

Breaks. The only thing you'd take a beatin' crossing the Breaks to come in on this way."

Sherill looked at the others. Lockwood's face was set enigmatically. Slim avoided his glance. He wished it had been the other way around, for Mitch Lockwood was the best man of the pair. He looked back at Ed again, letting out a slow sigh, drawling tiredly: —

"Finish it in a hurry, will you? I'm dead on my feet."

"And that ain't no lie, boss," Slim put in.

"Maybe it isn't," Ed stated softly and with more meaning than either Sherill or Slim had put to the words. He took his boots down now and leaned forward. "Know where you are, stranger?"

"Somewhere north of the Missouri."

"But exactly where?" When Sherill shook his head, Ed went on, "I'll tell you. And do you know why I'll tell you?" He again waited for that shake of the head, again supplied his own answer.

"Because you're not leaving here. Not ever."

The silence that followed his clipped words was unbroken for long seconds, until Sherill said, "That's a strong dose to hand a man when he's down on his luck."

14

"Is it?" Ed tapped the desk with a crooked forefinger. "You were sent down here by the Royal Canadian Mounted. Because a few Victoria branded horses have disappeared down this way."

"That's news to me."

Ed smiled and lifted his hands in a gesture of mild helplessness. He looked at Lockwood. "You know what to do with him," he said. He was through talking, his mind made up.

Over the short silence, Mitch Lockwood drawled, "Not me, Ed."

Ed's eyes betrayed their first real show of emotion. They showed a live anger as he looked at Lockwood. Then, strangely, he shrugged his bony shoulders, saying, "Suit yourself. Go tell Purdy I want him."

Lockwood stepped around Sherill and went out the door. And now Ed's glance avoided Sherill. Slim fidgeted nervously near the door, as though anxious to be out of this. The silence ran on heavily.

Finally Sherill stepped over to the desk, close to the wall and an inner door, the bracketed lamp directly over his head. "Look," he said, leaning with hands on the desk's edge. "I'm on a lonesome. I need help. Give me a job and watch me if you want."

Ed tilted back in the chair and clasped

15

his hands behind his head. He closed his eyes and smiled faintly in boredom. "No dice."

"Then have a man take me out of this country. Clear out."

"Hunh-uh." The eyes remained closed, the bored smile held.

Sherill sighed, the sound of his exhalation slurring against the stillness. He straightened lazily and reached up and snatched the lamp from its bracket, hurling it.

Ed was coming up out of the chair and trying to dodge when the lamp smashed into his chest. Sherill caught the image of Slim lifting his hand fast along his right side as the room went suddenly pitch-black.

He swung on Slim and pain lanced through his wrist as his knuckles crushed in the side of Slim's face. He lunged and collided with Slim's collapsing weight and his groping left hand closed on Slim's Colt's and wrenched it free. He sidestepped and threw his shoulder hard against the door, falling headlong through it as the latch tore loose. He had time to think, *Fast, make it fast!* before he hit the ground on his knees, letting his weight go forward and rolling.

A gun exploded deafeningly from the room behind and a burning pain scorched across the thick muscles of his back. He rolled to a crouch and turned and threw two quick shots through the door's black rectangle. On the heel of his shots, someone shouted down by the bunkhouse. He got to his feet and ran as hard as he could for the tie-rail.

He jerked loose the steeldust's reins and was lifting boot to stirrup when a gun winked rosily from the shadows before the bunkhouse. The horse's forelegs buckled and he went down, rolling into Sherill and bringing him to his knees, knocking his hat off. Sherill pulled his leg from under the thrashing animal and ran in on Lockwood's frightened rearing black.

He tore the reins loose, missed the stirrup and hung onto the horn as the mare wheeled away. He pulled himself up and went belly-down across the saddle, the animal breaking into a run. Guns were blasting the night behind him and he could hear Ed's voice as the wildly pitching mare carried him into the pines. He had a leg over when the black hit the creek. He had found the too-short stirrups by the time the mare ran through a gate and headed out the dimly visible line of a trail.

Lockwood's black had covered many miles during the day. An hour short of midnight she was completely played out. By that time she had carried Jim Sherill deep into a tangle

17

of hills to the west.

He staked out the mare and, taking quick inventory of the things in Lockwood's bed-roll, he ate some cold biscuits before pulling the tail of his shirt and running his hand along the bullet-burn on his back. It had stopped bleeding but was smarting painfully, enough to keep him awake a few minutes after he wrapped himself in the thin blanket and lay back against the saddle.

His last conscious thought was a gladness of being alive.

By noon of the next day, Jim Sherill was riding down out of the last gaunt tier of the badlands to the muddy banks of the Missouri, having covered better than forty miles since dawn. He waded the black across the wide stream and, in a grove of cotton-woods on the south bank, spent a solid hour.

First, he stripped and waded into the shallows and scrubbed himself as clean as he could without soap, gingerly washing his back-wound clean. He scrubbed most of the blood-stain from the tear at the back of his shirt. He shaved with Lockwood's straight-edge, grimacing with pain as the razor pulled at his stiff three-day-old beard. Then he built a fire.

Lockwood's bedroll produced jerky, more

cold biscuits, little else. He broiled several strips of jerky on the end of a green willow-branch and, with the biscuits, managed to dull the edge of his hunger. When he rode on he knew that the missing hat was the only thing that would call attention to his appearance.

That late afternoon, as he rode the main street into Whitewater, a tall and willowy girl did notice that he was hatless. But it was the black's shoulder-brand, not Sherill's bare-headedness, that first took her attention.

Studying this strange rider closely, she asked herself, *Have I seen him before?* She knew she hadn't.

Sure of this, a small excitement was growing in her as she hurried on along the walk. She had little difficulty keeping Jim Sherill in sight, for he was walking the black, taking his first look at the town.

He turned in to the tie-rail in front of the *Emporium,* took his time tying and glancing along the street, then crossed the awninged plank walk and went into the store. Coming along behind him, she noticed that he had to duck his head going through the door.

She followed him on back to the clothes-counter and stood behind him while he asked for a denim jumper, large size. Then a panic took her and she tried to think of something. In the end, she hurried up front and bought half a bolt of calico which, with the packages she was already carrying, more than filled her arms. She was back at the clothes-counter in time to see Sherill wearing the new jumper and trying on a wide gray Stetson with a curl-brim.

He bought the hat and paid for it and as he took his change and left the counter she came on past him and purposely let the bolt of cloth slip from under her arm.

It thudded heavily to the floor and when she turned, pretending to be startled, he was already reaching down for it. She smiled helplessly, trying to shift her packages to one hand, not succeeding and finally lifting an elbow, telling him, "Thank you. Please put it under my arm."

"Sort of loaded down, aren't you?" he asked with a broad grin.

He put the bolt under her arm and she let it slip again and he caught it as it fell. She laughed now and he liked the throatiness of her voice and the liveliness of her golden-brown eyes.

She shook her head and said half-angrily, "If I could only hold it tight enough. I really don't have far to carry it."

"Then you'd better let me help."

"Would you mind?" Her look was at once relieved. "It's only down the street."

He followed her out onto the walk and there, as they turned down-street, she told him, "You're very kind. I should have made two trips."

"Glad to help," he said.

They passed a bakery, a big livery-lot, a saloon where playing cards littered the plank walk, a barber-shop. He liked the way she lengthened her stride to match his and a couple of times he looked down at her, wondering if the slight uptilt to her nose heightened her prettiness or lessened it. She had a fine and sensitive face, and he decided he was wrong in thinking her pretty. Her good looks went beyond that. Her hair was the color of a sleek chestnut he had once owned. Her eyes were a lighter brown than his, her skin, the golden color of rich cream, had seen something of the sun.

They were coming up on a spired building he judged must be the courthouse when she asked, "Would you mind stopping in here with me for just a moment?" looking up at him with a half-smile.

"Anything you say, Miss," he drawled, and followed her in off the walk and through the building's nearest door.

It was an office, the back wall of which

was centered by a heavy steel door. A graying spare man with a nickeled five-pointed star pinned to his open vest came up out of a chair at a roll-top desk alongside the street window, saying cordially: —

"Now this is a nice surprise. How are you, Jean?"

"Hello, Fred." The girl laid her packages on the desk and turned to Sherill, holding out her hands, saying, "I'll take that now. It was nice of you to help me with it."

She lifted the bolt of calico out of his arms. She also lifted the Colt's from the belt of his waist-overalls.

She stepped quickly away from him, saying, "Sheriff, I want this man arrested."

Sheriff Fred Spence had given the youngster a quarter to find Ned Rawn. Not only the amount of money, but what he had seen back there in the sheriff's office had convinced the kid that his errand was important. So he hurried. He stopped at four or five places, first at Ned Rawn's office at the livery-lot, then at several saloons. He was out of breath when he looked in at the crowded bar of the *River House*.

He spotted Ned Rawn down at the far end, talking with a couple of men, and ran over and gave Rawn the sheriff's message,

22

adding, "You'd better hurry. Looks like trouble," in a wide-eyed way that made Rawn set his glass down without even waiting to empty it.

Ned Rawn gave the youngster a dime and hurried out. The courthouse was at the second cross-street above the river and on the way up there half a dozen people spoke to Rawn and one man tried to stop him. But he made his excuses pleasantly and went on. He was more accustomed to riding than walking and was breathless when he turned in at the door of the sheriff's office.

He saw Sherill first of all and the worried set of his thin face broke before an open-mouthed wonder. "Jim!" he breathed, grinning and coming over to shake Sherill's hand. "By God, it's good to see you!"

Only then did he see the girl standing a little to one side, and the pleasant smile he gave her and the way he touched his hat, saying politely, "How are you, Miss Ruick?" was in keeping with the neatly-pressed gray suit and his general well-groomed look.

He turned to the sheriff then. "So you'll have your fun, will you?" he said relievedly. "That kid had me worried, Fred. Said there was trouble."

"There is," the sheriff stated quietly. He

looked at the girl. "Tell Ned what you just told me, Jean."

At Rawn's look of puzzlement, Jean Ruick's head tilted up a little in defiance, as though she sensed that the odds were no longer in her favor. "This man rode one of our horses into town," she said, looking at Sherill. "He can't say how he got it, or he won't. I'm having him arrested."

Ned Rawn looked at Sherill, who drawled, "To begin with, Ned, it's a mare and not a horse."

Rawn saw the anger that flared in the girl's eyes and quickly said, "Jim Sherill a horse thief?" He laughed. Then sobering, he went on, "There's been some mistake. I've known Jim for ten years. We rode for the same outfit."

"Which proves nothing," Jean Ruick said coolly. "Make him explain why he was riding the Major's horse. Or mare," she added, glaring at Sherill.

Rawn looked at his friend. "Go on, Jim. Tell her."

"I already have. She won't believe it."

"Let's have it again," the sheriff said mildly. He eased down into the chair at the desk now, obviously reserving judgment in a way Ned Rawn knew was typical of him. Old Fred Spence was a shrewd man and pretty generally a straight thinker.

"It's like I said," Sherill stated. "Last night a pair of hard cases hit my camp down along the river, held a gun on me and went through my things. They took around forty dollars, a watch and my gelding, a bay. The bay was in good shape and this mare they left me was done in. They hadn't found my forty-five hid in one of my boots. I made the mistake of pullin' it too soon as they went away and got this for my trouble." Turning, he lifted the back of his new copper-riveted jumper and showed Rawn the tear and the faded blood-stain on his shirt.

"Where was this?" Fred Spence wanted to know.

"Twenty, twenty-five miles down the river."

"It took you a long time to get here."

"It took the mare a long time, not me, Sheriff. She's been used pretty hard."

Spence folded his arms on the desk and looked across at the girl. "Well, Jean?"

"Do you believe all this?" she asked uncertainly.

He shrugged his spare shoulders. "Think I do. Chiefly because Ned knows him."

"That means nothing to me," she said defensively.

"If it don't, then swear out a warrant. I'll hold him."

"Miss Ruick," Rawn put in patiently. "This man's a responsible person. If necessary, I'll put up his bail. Now why not be reasonable?"

She avoided his glance, looking at the sheriff, undecided and now more embarrassed than angry.

Fred Spence told her, "Suppose I keep an eye on him? If he skips town, we'll go after him."

"That's ridiculous, Fred," Rawn said. "Jim's doin' business with the Army. Suppose he has to go somewhere? Fort Selby, for instance."

"What kind of business?" Spence looked at Sherill.

"Freight," Sherill blandly answered, and the law man missed Rawn's hastily-concealed start of surprise.

"You could drop in here and tell me when you were leaving and how long you'd be gone, couldn't you?" Spence asked.

Sherill nodded.

"That suit you, Jean?"

The girl gave a reluctant nod and Spence, much relieved, picked up the bolt of calico and walked with her to the door, telling her, "Maybe you ought to be thankful you got the mare back and let it go at that, Jean." They stepped outside and Rawn and

26

Sherill didn't catch her reply as the street noises blurred her voice.

Rawn shot his tall friend a frowning glance, acidly drawling, "Freight!" and Sherill's lean face took on a sheepish grin.

Shortly, the sheriff came back into the room, went to his desk and picked up Sherill's gun. As he handed it across, he said, "She's leaving your saddle at Kramer's livery." He glanced at Rawn, adding, "Sorry about this, Ned. But she was pretty steamed up. How's horse tradin'?"

"So-so," Rawn conceded.

Spence followed them as far as the door. "Better stop around tomorrow, Sherill. Someone else may have bumped into that pair. Make it around eight if you're up this way."

"I'll do that," Sherill said, and he and Rawn went on down the walk.

These two were old friends and now, as they approached the corner below the courthouse, Sherill impulsively threw an arm around Rawn's shoulder and good-naturedly shook him, drawling, "Still the same shadbellied, fancy-dressin' son of a gun. Ned, you look prosperous."

Rawn shrugged the arm away, trying to look serious but not quite managing it. "Freight," he said acidly, using the same tone he had in the jail.

He looked up at Sherill, trying to tell if there were changes in him. There were none he could notice beyond a certain maturity of the face. This Jim Sherill was still the same, a man generous in every physical proportion and, Rawn knew, also generously gifted in the qualities that drew others to him. There was a fine-drawn look about him, a rawhide toughness that Rawn remembered well and envied a little.

Just now Sherill laughed softly, saying, "You should've seen the way she roped me in there, Ned. Prettiest thing you ever saw. Who is she?"

"Jean Ruick." Rawn was faintly amused. "Quite a catch. Brains. And looks, as you saw."

"And plenty of fire." Sherill spoke almost gravely. "Who's the Major she mentioned?"

"Caleb Donovan, her uncle. He runs the outfit for her." Rawn was thinking of something else and added wryly, "Fred Spence can check your story on the freight. How much of the rest was the truth?"

"You saw my shirt."

"Was that all?"

Sherill looked around, chuckling softly, saying, "Just about."

"I thought so," Rawn said in disgust.

They were now abreast the *River House's*

broad veranda. Beyond a lower warehouse, Sherill could see a broad expanse of the cluttered levee and the river. The paddle-wheel and then the after-decks of a stately river boat gradually came into view. Sherill guessed her name even before he left Rawn and walked on a few steps, far enough to see the towering twin stacks and the wheelhouse with the legend *Queen* lettered along its side.

A wide smile was on his lean face as he came back to his friend. "So they're still here?" he asked.

Rawn nodded. "Right here. Upstairs."

His seriousness relaxed at seeing the excitement that brightened Sherill's look and he followed his friend up the steps and into the lobby, asking in mock-seriousness, "What's the rush?" For Sherill was walking fast now.

They crossed the ornate lobby and climbed the stairs, Sherill two steps at a time and then impatiently waiting at the upper landing as Rawn purposely dawdled.

"Which room, Ned?"

"Front end of the hall."

Rawn waited there, leaning on the banister as Sherill went along the dark and uncarpeted hallway. He heard Sherill's knock up there.

"No one in," Sherill called disappointedly after a few seconds.

"Try the other two, twelve and fourteen. They've got the whole front end."

Rawn listened as Sherill knocked once more, then presently again. Finally Sherill came back along the narrow corridor saying, "No luck."

"They're probably out eating. We'll go down to my room."

"I could stand some soap and water," Sherill said. He followed Rawn to a room at the back of the hall and, as his friend pushed the door open, asked, "How is she, Ned?"

"Fine." Seeing the look on Sherill's face, Rawn added, "Thank God the bug's never bitten me."

He took a towel from a hook behind the door and nodded to the pitcher and basin on the marble-topped washstand. "Help yourself," he said, and crossed over and sat on the bed, his thin frame all angles.

"Now let's have it," he said. "From the beginning."

Sherill pulled off his shirt, the white skin of his ropy-muscled shoulders and arms a decided contrast to sun-blackened face and neck and hands. "What happened at this end?" he wanted to know.

"I paid off your crew two weeks ago and they pulled out the next day after one hell of a sweet spree. The horses were delivered and collected on, except for your two geldings. Kramer's holding them. I banked the money for you."

"That helps."

Rawn sighed audibly. "All right, keep me guessin'! You wind up with a quarter of what you should've had and all you say is it helps. Talk, man! Your foreman said you'd gone up into the Breaks alone. What took you so damned long?"

"Riding a stage up to Canada and coming into that country the back way."

"What good did that do you?"

Sherill was lathering his face and neck as he replied, "Don't know yet."

"Then you're just where you started. A guy who's lost sixty horses and thinks he can get 'em back without any help." Rawn was plainly disgusted.

"Maybe it'll pay off." Sherill reached for the towel. "I bought a cast-off horse from the police up there. They put me onto a hideout near the line that they've been watching and I lay over there two days, keeping an eye on it. Finally a couple of jaspers showed up at this place. That night I swapped my spavined jughead for one of theirs."

"Then what?" Rawn was sitting up now, intent on what Sherill was saying.

"They lit out after me and I tolled 'em down through the mountains a couple days. Yesterday they corraled me and brought me down to their layout. It was too dark to be sure, but I think I saw my horses."

"You think?" Rawn's tone was deflated. "Then you're not sure of anything. Why didn't you go in from this end and save all that time?"

"After swingin' a sticky loop on a big bunch of horses, wouldn't they be expecting someone from this end?"

"All right, I can see that," Rawn said grudgingly. "But you're here and your horse-string is still up in the hills."

"I'll go back."

"Alone?"

Sherill nodded. He was pulling on his shirt.

"Can you? Did they just let you walk out of there?"

"Not quite." Sherill was half smiling and he repeated, "Not quite."

Rawn shook his head worriedly. "I'd go to Fred Spence and tell him the whole thing, Jim."

"Why? From what those outfits down south had to say, the law up here has never dared to take a posse into that country. And plenty of cattle and horses have strayed in there. Not on their own, either."

"So you handed Spence a trumped-up story. You're wrong about him. He's a good man. Honest."

"And careful."

Rawn smiled crookedly and said in a dry way, "You're still the same. You'll get the bit in your teeth and never let go."

"Should I?"

"This time, yes." Rawn leaned forward now, wagging a finger in emphasis as he said, "Give it up, Jim. There's a dozen easier ways of making up your losses. I'm your friend, so use me. In ninety days I make another remount delivery. Spend that time combin' the country, buyin' horse-flesh. I'll pay you a hundred and ten a head and take every sound animal you can lay hands on. In the end you'll be ahead. Way ahead. And," he added significantly, "alive."

Sherill's level glance was still on him. "You've made other commitments for that contract, Ned."

"Suppose I have?" Rawn shrugged. "What do those men mean to me? Not a damned thing. You do. So I reject enough of the others to handle your stuff."

A wondering look crossed Sherill's face. He turned away, afraid that Rawn might see how he felt. He picked up his jumper and put it on. A lot of his elation ove seeing Rawn was gone now.

"Well, how about it?" Rawn asked.

Sherill had a bad moment trying to think of something non-committal to say, something that wouldn't hurt Rawn's feelings. Finally it came, and he drawled, "If you were short on this last delivery because of me, why wouldn't the Army let you make up the shortage next time?"

"They would. But we're talkin' about another thing. About a damn' sight more than the sixty head you lost. You'll really cash in."

Sherill wasn't liking this and was trying not to show it. He was embarrassed and irritated at the change he saw in Ned Rawn. Three years ago, when he'd last seen his friend, Ned would have been even more red-headed than he over a thing like losing these horses. Ned had been wild and a born gambler and maybe a little unreliable at times. But he'd also been straight as a string. And there was nothing straight about this.

From the hallway just now sounded the unrhythmic tread of someone, more than one person, coming up the stairs out of the lobby. Sherill was thankful for the interruption, for the excuse it gave him to go to the door and open it and look up along the hallway.

He hadn't expected it would be them. But

there they were, just turning out of the head of the stairs.

He called, "Ruth!" and she and her father stopped.

He walked quickly along the corridor and up to her, laughing softly and delightedly at her look of utter surprise.

He took Ruth Lovelace in his arms and lifted her from the floor and swung her completely around. Then he kissed her full on the lips, while beside them George Lovelace beamed proudly and said in a voice that boomed, "Son, we thought you'd forgotten us. Let me shake your hand."

Ruth pushed her shoulders away from Sherill, laughing and saying, "Jim, you're cutting me in two!" He put her down and then shook hands with her father.

Commodore George Lovelace, the origin of whose title was somewhat obscure, pumped Sherill's hand and affably said, "This is a great day for us, son. God A'mighty, you're big! Must've grown a couple inches this past year."

"He's just right, Dad." Ruth pressed Sherill's arm that was about her waist, giving him her brightest smile.

The Commodore looked on past them now at Rawn, who stood in the door to his room. "Ned, we've got something to celebrate," he called. "Come along and we'll find a drink."

"You three go on and have your fun," Rawn answered. "See you after supper."

"Sure you can't come?" the Commodore asked. He caught Rawn's shake of the head and told him, "Then we'll count on you after supper."

The Commodore was turning away when Rawn called, "Hang on a minute, Jim." He stepped back into the room and a moment later reappeared and came along the hallway carrying Sherill's new Stetson. When Sherill came on a few steps to take it from him, he said low-voiced, "You lucky devil!" and was broadly smiling as Sherill rejoined Ruth.

"Now come along, you two." George Lovelace led the way up the hall.

He was a short and rotund man, silver-haired, tonight wearing a black suit with polished brass buttons. Whiskey, not the sun, was responsible for the redness of his full, round face. He had a pompous, hearty manner that now prompted him to make a small ceremony of opening the door, and ushering them into the over-furnished living room of his suite.

"Tom!" he bawled as he closed the door. Without waiting for an answer, he turned to Ruth. "Where's that good for nothing nigger?"

"Comin', suh. Comin'," a husky voice answered from beyond an archway leading off the front of the room, and shortly a colored boy of twelve or thirteen appeared in the thickening shadows there.

"Tom, this is Jim Sherill. From now on he's one of the family. And don't you forget it." Lovelace used his most imperious tone on his servant.

He waited until the boy bobbed his kinky head and then, with a wave of the hand, told him, "Now hike on down to the boat and bring us two or three bottles of champagne. Cold, mind you. And I'll thrash your black hide if you don't hurry."

"Yes, suh!" The boy gave Sherill and Ruth a toothy grin and hurried out the door.

"Now, Jim. Tell us about your trip." Lovelace slapped Sherill on the back.

"There's not much to tell," Sherill said.

His eye was on the girl, his year-long hunger for the sight of her making him momentarily ignore the Commodore. She was golden-haired and had a round and pretty face, full-cheeked like her father's. The blue dress that so closely matched the color of her eyes was tight-gathered at the waist, showing the strongly feminine contours of her small body. She seemed quieter than he remembered, less a girl and more a woman.

"Ned said you wouldn't be back till you'd found the horses and hung the thieves," Lovelace said, insistent at having Sherill's attention. "I trust you've banked all that gold and aren't letting it lie around somewhere under your saddle."

He caught the sober look that touched Sherill's face and drew back a little, at once asking, "Something wrong, son?"

"Not much, Commodore. I've found the horses, but they're still up in the hills."

Lovelace was startled. He laughed uneasily. "But ready to bring down, of course?"

"Not quite."

"Then those cutthroats still have them?"

Sherill nodded. "They do. But not for long, I hope."

The Commodore's worried look eased somewhat. "You'll call on the sheriff this time, won't you, son?"

"No. Thought I'd give it another try on my own first."

"Jim, you can't!" Ruth breathed, alarm in her eyes. "That's taking a dreadful chance."

"This is worth taking a chance on, Ruth."

A glance Sherill didn't understand passed between them and Lovelace turned away and walked to the front of the room and began pacing back and forth before the dusk-darkened window overlooking the street. Ruth

38

stepped over to the table alongside a heavy horsehair sofa and lit the pink-globed lamp there and then sat down.

As the light drove back the shadows, Sherill sensed a change of feeling in both of them, a change that flattened the heady enjoyment of this meeting. He said, a little awkwardly, "This will work itself out. If it doesn't, there's still enough left to pay back that loan, Commodore."

"That thousand be damned!" Lovelace flared angrily. "The profits from it were to have been a wedding present to you two," he announced bluntly. "I wasn't going to mention it."

"There's still a good chance I'll get the herd back, Sir," Sherill told him, warned to mildness by that danger-signal of Lovelace's rising temper.

"But suppose the horses are gone for good?"

Sherill lifted his wide shoulders. "I can try again next year."

The Commodore ran a hand over his face, thoughtfully studying Sherill. "Next year Ruth will be twenty-two. You're nearly thirty."

"Twenty-seven."

Lovelace nodded. "Time you two were raising a family. Ruth's mother had her when she was eighteen."

"Dad, don't be coarse," Ruth murmured.

"It's the truth, isn't it? A southern girl can't be far in her twenties and have many eligible young men very interested in her."

"Ruth isn't having to worry about that." There was an edge to Sherill's voice.

"Don't be too sure," Lovelace said, his face redder than it had been. "This was to be the year you made your money. You were to put the ranch in the hands of some good man and come hack to Hannibal with us. You were to buy into the business and start learning it so you could take over from me."

"That can still happen, Commodore."

"Can it? You've been gone three weeks, the Lord knows where, since we had the word you'd lost those horses. What've you done? You're back here now without a thing."

"Give me a few more days," Sherill said evenly, crowding back his anger. "Say a week."

"But suppose you don't have any luck?"

"Then I still have enough to get along on. A little in the bank, a few head of cattle down in Wyoming on the layout. We'll be all right, won't we, Ruth?"

She looked up at him with a smile that

wasn't convincing. "I hardly know what to say, Jim."

Lovelace laughed in a dry way. "Have Ruth come out here and live like some filthy Cree squaw? Not on your life."

"What's wrong . . ."

"She couldn't stand this life," the Commodore cut in. "Why, man, she's been raised to have everything. Spoiled rotten, she is. And it's my fault. But facts are facts and there they are."

"Isn't that up to her?" Sherill asked evenly.

A livid anger flushed Lovelace's face to tell Sherill, too late, of his mistake.

"It damn' well isn't up to her!" the Commodore burst out. "Sir, I'll have you know I won't stand for such talk! Here I've offered you everything but the shirt off my back, practically handed over my business to you. And you have the gall to question my authority!"

"No one's questioning it. But Ruth should have something . . ."

"Ruth's my daughter, Sherill. She's been raised to mind her elders."

"She's of age, Commodore," Sherill said, thinking, *He can't do this to me, to us,* and he went on, "She's able to decide this for herself."

Lovelace's look became apoplectic. He was

41

about to say something when the door opened and the colored boy came in, three big bottles filling his skinny arms.

George Lovelace swung around, saw who it was and bellowed, "Take that damned stuff away!"

The boy, frightened, hastily backed out of the door. Then the Commodore faced Sherill again, his jaw set tightly. "So you're already trying to run my household, are you?"

"Look, Sir," Sherill said with all the patience he could command. "All I'm asking is that you wait and see how I make out. If worst comes to worst, Ruth and I can still get along."

"I won't allow Ruth to marry an ordinary cowhand and live in this God-forsaken country."

Sherill eyed the man levelly, drawling, "We'll see."

"You'll see what?"

"We'll see how my luck runs." Sherill looked at Ruth now. "Do I get another chance?"

"I . . . I think we should wait," she said, quite helplessly. "Can't we talk about it later, Jim?"

"We'll talk when Sherill shows up with those horses." Deliberately, Lovelace crossed over to the door and picked up Sherill's hat from the chair alongside it. His look was narrow-eyed and angry as he extended the hat. "Not before, Sherill. Is that plainly understood?"

Only now did Jim Sherill fully realize the corner into which the Commodore had crowded him. Fear struck through him, a fear of nothing physical but of realizing that his future lay in the balance, weighed against this man's unreasoning and unstable temper. Tonight was setting a pattern for the rest of their lives. Lovelace wouldn't soon forget this, would never forgive a thing that had been said. He should have humored the man, Sherill knew, should have let him have his own way, taken his abuse without standing up to it.

Knowing all these things, he took his hat from the Commodore, nodded to Ruth and opened the door.

"We'll expect better word from you next time we see you, Sherill," Lovelace said, adding pointedly, "or there won't be a next time."

His words goaded Jim Sherill over that last edge of reason and into real and unforgiving anger. Sherill stood there in the doorway with a smile slowly coming to his face. Finally he laughed.

"Do you see anything amusing about this?"

Lovelace asked in an aloof, cold-angry way.

Sherill nodded. "You can't keep her shut up under lock and key, Commodore."

He turned away and walked to the head of the stairs, Lovelace calling after him, "We'll see about that!" He was halfway down the stairs when he heard the door slam with a violence that thundered along the corridor.

Standing in the deepening dusk on the veranda, he absent-mindedly rolled a smoke and then stood without lighting it, feeling his anger cool, regret beginning to crowd him. He asked himself tiredly if he and Ruth were ever again to be together in that carefree and utterly happy association that had been theirs until now. He doubted it.

He wondered about eating but relished the thought of food even less than he had that of the tobacco. He took the cigarette from his mouth as he heard someone open the screen door behind him. He edged over and away from the head of the steps.

"Jim!"

Ruth's voice softly calling his name brought him swinging around. She was standing close and now she came against him with a violence that crushed the cigarette in his hand. Her arms were around him then, and she kissed him with a gusty and passionate abandon.

Afterward, she drew away quickly, saying

with a careful emphasis on each word, "Jim, don't ever take what Dad says as being what I think."

Then, before he could recover from his surprise, she turned and left him.

II

The day before, in the late afternoon, shortly after Lockwood and Slim had made Sherill their prisoner, Jake Henry's curiosity had been roused by stray sounds shuttling up out of a ravine directly below him. The sounds Henry soon identified as belonging to several horses on the move and, out of curiosity at encountering anyone in this isolated spot, he rode on to a point where the ravine opened out, all the while keeping high along the timbered ridge flanking it.

So presently he had watched three riders come out of the trees below. He knew all three. One he had frequently seen on his occasional prowls through these southward hills. The second belonged with the first, although he was a comparative stranger. The third, Jake hadn't seen for two years. It was this third man, Sherill, that his glance clung to unbelievingly at first, then in anger.

He had kept his distance as he went on and an hour later widely circled the high meadow above the big corral, which he guessed rightly to be the destination of the trio. He and his mule made camp several miles below the hill-ranch and therefore he didn't hear the shots. His bleak mood would have been a good bit relieved had he heard them.

As it was, thinking about Jim Sherill stirred the bile in him to the point where he couldn't sleep for better than an hour after hitting his blanket, casting back over certain things pretty strongly imprinted on his keen memory.

During the morning he'd still been thinking about that third man and finally, after breakfast, he saddled the mule and headed south through the timber in the general direction of the river. He had farther to ride than Sherill and it took him longer to reach Whitewater. He rode into the town at dusk, a long-haired and rangy, buckskin-clad shape astride the big mule.

He spent half an hour in the *Merchandise* buying supplies, paying in gold-dust, arranging to call for his goods the following morning. It was dark when he rode on up and turned his mule into Kramer's corral and afterward entered the first saloon he came to along the street, the *Fine and Dandy*.

The place was crowded and noisy and the air reeked of stale smoke and of whiskey. From the rear sounded the tinny din of a

47

piano and the talk and laughter were pitched to a high note. Jake considered the long crowded bar only momentarily before his pale eyes took on an amused glint.

Without further ceremony, he made his way forward through the crowd by using hands and elbows and shoulders, ungently moving men out of his way. Two or three protested violently before thinking better of it. Jake Henry was a full head taller than any man in the room and he ignored all these complaints with an unaffected boredom.

"Whiskey. A jug," he told one of the aprons.

He paid and made his way toward the back of the room, the half-gallon crockery jug dangling from his left hand. He found a small table unoccupied beyond the back poker layout and took it. He uncorked the jug and drank thirstily, grimacing at the bite of the fiery liquid.

Presently the piano stopped its discordant beat and the couples on the dance-floor drifted away from it. One medium-tall man, heavy-set, and with a coarse face, brought a house-girl over to Jake's table and, scowling down, said gruffly, "Move out. That table's ours."

Jake moved no more than his eyes, which lifted to stare impassively at the man a long moment. "Go 'way," he finally drawled, and dropped his eyes again.

The other's blunt jaw thrust out and he took a step toward Jake. But this put him within view of the long-barreled Navy Colt's and the knife hanging from the belt bisecting Jake's long buckskin jacket. He hastily revised his intention, said to the girl, "Hell! Let's drink," and turned and took her over to the bar.

Jake had another long pull at the jug, then another, relishing this sop to a conceit that told him he could still, having just turned forty, outwalk or outride or outfight or outshoot any man he had ever known, white or Indian. He would sometimes qualify this blanket assumption by uneasily remembering one exception to it. But generally it was his belief that he was the best man alive.

His profession called for such certainties, for he was of that seldom-seen breed known as the "wolfer." A preference for his own company, plus a liking for solitude, plus the Territory's generous bounty on wolf heads had led Jake Henry into his way of life.

A Kentucky upbringing had given him an extraordinary skill with firearms, successfully deserting the Confederate Army and hiding out for a year had strengthened his natural distrust of most men, and roaming the uninhabited regions of Wyoming and Idaho, and now Montana, had made him independent as a crow. He had been hunted by the Indians and in turn had hunted them. Seven years ago he had burned his collection of scalps as representing something he had gone stale on, a sport for which he no longer had any zest.

Four or five times each year he would leave the hills and come down to trading post or settlement, buy supplies and ammunition and get drunk. Each of these visits sickened him to the point where he foreswore any further contact with his fellow man. But loneliness and his appetite for drink always drew him back again.

Now, consuming whiskey as fast as the muscle-spasms in his stomach would let him, he idly kept an eye on the man who had tried to take his table. Presently he noticed that that individual had left the girl and was standing near the front of the bar talking with a barrel-chested house-man and two less savory characters. Occasionally one of them would glance back at him and quickly away again.

Jake was delighted at the prospects. For the first time in twenty-four hours his reason for going on this spree was forgotten.

A quarter-hour later, when the quartette

began slowly working its way toward him through the crowd, half the whiskey in the jug was beginning to explode in his brain. He didn't watch them now.

They split into pairs, each pair unobtrusively edging in his direction, one or the other now and then stopping to listen to the music or to look in on a poker game or simply to stand idly staring at nothing in particular.

When the house-man stood ten feet away, within easy range, Jake suddenly lunged erect, picked up his chair and threw it.

They rushed him then. All but the house-man, who couldn't.

Jake met their rush by kicking the table into them. One man went down, bawling loudly in pain at a pair of scraped shins. A ripple of excitement ran along the room and someone up front let out a shout.

The next moment the more timid element in the crowd headed for the swing doors and boiled out onto the walk, causing a jam there. Then, gathering courage and numbers, they turned and tried to push their way back into the saloon again. The stream of movement along the walk slowed, stopped and finally spilled into the street.

By the time Jim Sherill came along, just having left the *River House,* wheel-traffic was snarled and the driver of a high-bodied freight had his six teams tangled with those of the Arrow Creek stage stalled in front of him.

Sherill left the walk, ducked under the tie-rail and was winding his way through the crowd when a roar of voices rolled out of the saloon. Only mildly curious, he stopped and looked over the churning mass of heads and through the saloon's wide open doors.

He saw Jake Henry's shaggy head towering over the others at the smoke-fogged room's back wall and instantly recognized the wolfer. A strong urgency hit him at sight of a bleeding gash on Jake's right cheek. Just then Jake's mighty bellow sounded over the general din and he saw the wolfer step out and swing a chair-leg club and dodge quickly back to the wall again.

Sherill didn't wait for more but pushed roughly into the crowd, his long arms sweeping men aside. Once he said, "Sorry, neighbor," as he wedged a shoulder between two men and twisted them roughly apart. He elbowed aside a man leaning against one of the doors and then, braced against it, forced his way into the saloon.

Another strident yell of Jake's wiped out the last of Sherill's caution and he went the length of the room not caring who he jarred or shouldered aside. One man swung on him,

52

missed, and a second later backed quickly away with a face stinging from an open-handed swipe. Sherill used elbows, boots, shoulders and fists and shortly, well winded, he stood among the men who blocked off the corner in which Jake Henry stood.

It was worse than it had looked from outside. Four men faced Jake inside the fifteen-foot space ringed by the crowd. The houseman was definitely out of it with a badly sprained shoulder which he gripped tightly with his good hand. Of the remaining three, the burly one whose table Jake had stolen stood spraddle-legged and with the jagged neck-end of a broken bottle in his fist, a skinned cheek-bone and a swollen eye the only marks on him. Of the other pair, the shorter and stockier had a scalp-cut that was bleeding down the back of his neck, a ripped vest that hung in tatters, a mashed mouth. The remaining man stood as far as he could from Jake, hunched over with both arms across his middle and not the slightest trace of color on his face.

Sherill had seen Jake looking better. But nevertheless Jake now wiped the blood from his cheek and brandished his club with a reddened arm that lifted from the ribbons of a torn buckskin sleeve, saying dryly:

"Quit the dancin' and let's mix it, boys."

He seemed to be having trouble focusing his eyes, which were bright with a glaze easy to recognize. Nearby, in the splintered remains of a table, lay the broken shards of Jake's jug. His moccasined feet stood in a puddle of whiskey. From an empty lamp-bracket on the wall behind him hung his wide belt, knife and gun dangling from it.

He's having his fun in the same old way was Sherill's thought. A tingling anticipation ran through him as he looked at the wolfer. Strangely, the energy he had spent fighting his way the length of the room seemed to have burnt out the deep core of depression he had carried away from his meeting with Lovelace. He was feeling good now, more alive and at ease with himself.

The crowd was quiet, tense and waiting. The burly man, still looking at Jake, spoke out the side of his mouth and quite softly said, "This time, Black," and a shorter thick-chested individual close to Sherill answered just as softly, "Let 'er rip, Sid."

Shortly Sid took a quick step at Jake, then dodged sideways and in. Jake's club swished down and the crowd let out a roar. Jake missed and so did Sid's sudden stab with the jagged bottle. But now Jake's side was to Sherill. Black, seeing his chance, lunged in.

Sherill reached out with a boot and tripped Black, calling, "Watch it, Jake!" as the man sprawled headlong. The wolfer turned and Black scrambled back out of the way.

Sherill half-smiled as he looked down at Black, drawling, "Better wait your turn."

Black picked himself up, glaring at Sherill, and Jake sidled away from Sid and looked this way, asking loudly, "Who yelled then?"

"I did, Jake."

The wolfer squinted and finally saw Sherill. A glad smile touched his hawkish face. But then a quick reserve settled over it and his voice intoned, "Who the hell're you?" in a rough-edged belligerence.

"You remember," Sherill stepped into the cleared area beyond the crowd.

Jake's attention was altogether on Sherill. Sid saw that and lunged. At the last moment Jake saw him coming and lifted his club. Sid let out a howl of pain lost in the crowd's excited roar as the club caught him under the wrist, knocking the bottle from his down-sweeping hand. Then Jake swung with his left and his fist caught Sid hard on the ear and knocked him into the wall. But for a moment Jake's back was exposed, and now Black and the one with the torn vest rushed him.

Sherill caught Black by the arm, swung

him around and hit him solidly at the hinge of the jaw. Black's weight collapsed into him as someone jumped him from behind. A man darted from the jam-packed fringe of the circle and tried to pull the interloper off Sherill and still another onlooker hit this one.

The sudden violence was like a tonic to Sherill. He was relishing this moment and let his pent-up feelings boil over in a furious burst of energy that seemed instantly to cleanse him of all the poisonous disappointment and frustration and humiliation this evening had brought.

An angry roar rolled back across the room now. At the bar an apron, understanding this telltale sign, went pasty-faced and reached under the counter to swing up a sawed-off Greener. He lifted the shot-gun, pulled both triggers and the thunderous double-concussion blew the lid off. Violence spread like a grass fire before a high wind.

Men with no thought of a quarrel turned and started clawing and gouging and kicking their way to safety. They were slugged and before they knew it were slugging back. Both bar lamps were shattered by thrown bottles and the long bar mirror splintered and came down in a heavy jangling that rode musically over the din. Voices roared in profanity and fear and just plain exuberance.

In that back corner, Sherill had spread his boots wide and bent far over, arching his back suddenly to throw the man who had jumped him. The man's cartwheeling frame slammed into Sid and they both went down and Jake deliberately turned and with a roundhouse swing flattened the last man of the original quartette who had hesitated too long near him.

A broad grin of sheer enjoyment was on Sherill's face as he saw a man coming at him from the side. He wheeled in alongside Jake, yelling, "Let's beat it, friend!" The wolfer swung his club viciously, flooring Sherill's antagonist. Suddenly a chair hurtled over the heads of the crowd ten feet away, bringing down the shaded lamp over the back poker layout and throwing this corner in near darkness.

Beside Sherill, Jake growled, "Get the hell away from me, stranger!"

"Wake up, Jake. You know me," Sherill answered. He vaguely saw a shape diving in at the wolfer and threw himself at it, his knees catching the man in the chest, bringing the wind from his lungs in a choked groan.

Someone piled into Sherill and he threw a savage uppercut that missed. A down man's swinging legs tripped him and he sprawled full length. He lost his hat, found it again.

He had to fight his way to his feet and as the last lamp up front guttered out he had a fleeting glimpse of Jake slugging and working his way out of the corner and up along the wall.

Sherill fought his way quickly to the wall and shortly came abreast a waist-high window, calling loudly, "Here we go, Jake!" He made out the wolfer's high shape directly ahead against the feeble light shining in from the street. He got a hold on Jake's arm and felt it jerked away.

Jake was drunk, evidently too drunk even to remember him. The wolfer had started this near-riot and, enjoyable as it had been, it was now time to be getting out of here.

Knowing this, Sherill did what he thought he had to, very deliberately, carefully.

He stepped over to Jake, took a hold on his arm and suddenly pulled him off-balance. Then he hit him, hit hard. His blow was low and merely staggered the wolfer. He swung again, and this time his knuckles ached against the shelving slope of Jake's jaw. He saw the tall man's shape melt down and out of sight.

He stooped and there Jake lay. He gripped him under the arms and lifted him toward the window, staggering into the wall as someone collided with him. At the window he kicked the glass from the lower sash, threw Jake belly down across the sill, and shoved him on out. Then he went out after him, falling against the adjoining building.

Jake lay there huddled in the trash of the narrow alleyway. Sherill awkwardly lifted the wolfer across his shoulder and walked back from the street. He reached the back alley and turned up along it, hearing the muffled roar of the fight through the saloon's thin wall. Something kept slapping the back of his thighs. It was Jake's belt and gun and knife. Somehow, in the confusion back there, Jake had managed to remember them.

A hundred yards up the alley Sherill stopped to rest. Now most of the noise was coming from the street. He picked Jake up again and went on. The wolfer was out cold, breathing loudly, a dead weight.

He came to a darkened cross-street, saw that it was clear and lurched across it. Behind the street-fronting buildings was a barn and corral with a windmill on its alley side. There was a log trough inside the corral and Sherill dumped Jake's loose weight through the poles and then tiredly climbed through. He dragged the wolfer over to the trough and pulled the belt from his hand, tossing the weapons aside. Then he got Jake to his knees and sloshed water into his face.

Jake gagged but didn't lift his head. So Sherill hoisted him higher and pushed his head into the trough and held it under the water a few seconds. When the wolfer began thrashing and pushing, Sherill let him go and stepped back out of the way.

Jake sat there looking up at him dazedly a moment. Then the wolfer reached up and pulled himself to his moccasined feet. He had to spread his feet wide to stand. Even so, he was taller than Sherill.

"Better now?" Sherill asked.

In this faint light he could see Jake's shoulders hunch over. Suddenly Jake stepped in and swung at him. He easily dodged the blow and watched Jake stumble and go to his knees.

He laughed, drawling, "Brother, you must've taken on a load."

"Not too much to keep me from handlin' you." Jake's tone was brittle with anger. With some difficulty, he came to his feet again, breathing, "Y' licked me once. But never again. Not this time!"

"Jake, you're out on your feet," Sherill said patiently. "The law's lookin' for you. I can't turn you loose this way."

"The law!" Jake scoffed. "What the hell should you know about the law?"

"Not much, Jake."

"But you will," the wolfer breathed in seeming irrelevance. "The whole damned rotten pack of you will, some day. Ed Stedman! You're travellin' with a high-grade outfit, Sherill. Now I'll beat some sense into your head."

Suddenly Sherill understood what was the matter with Jake; or rather, he understood part of it.

A long laugh welled up out of his wide chest and when Jake, angrier than ever now, took a lurching step toward him, he let the wolfer almost reach him and suddenly ducked down and wheeled in behind him. He straightened with his arms around Jake's waist. He lifted Jake and tilted him sideways and threw him on his face.

There was a three-second interval when he let go his hold and Jake seemed about to thrash free. But finally he had his knees on Jake's shoulders and the wolfer's arms drawn up behind his back, wrists crossed.

"Who was goin' to beat sense into whose head?" Sherill drawled.

Then he proceeded to tell Jake a few things.

The next morning, in the loft of the barn alongside the windmill where Sherill had given Jake his soaking, a hostler's loud whistling of *Tenting Tonight* brought Sherill awake. He lay there unmoving in the darkness, listening to the tune and the swishing of the hay as the hostler pitched his forkfuls from the loft door down into the corral. Shortly, a lantern's light laid sweeping shadows against the roof's planking and Sherill heard steps going down a ladder. Then the loft was left in darkness.

Sherill sat up, stifling a groan as pain stabbed at his side. He pulled on his boots, taking inventory of the damage to his big frame. In addition to the sore ribs and the bullet-burn along his back, the knuckles of his right hand were tender and there was a kink in his left side. He grinned into the darkness, musing, *fair enough,* warmly thinking back upon last night's heady excitement.

He could hear Jake's even breathing off there in the blackness to his left and considered waking the wolfer, finally deciding against it. He remembered that somehow he had managed to hang onto the new Stetson throughout the brawl and now, groping around, he found it and slid down into the empty end of the loft.

He went to the big door and looked out across the roofs of the town, seeing a faint grayness beginning to show along the uneven horizon to the east. The stars were beginning to pale out, gray banners of smoke lifted from a few chimneys and a rooster's crowing echoed in from the edge of town. He climbed down the outside ladder from the loft door and headed for the alley and the windmill trough, shivering a little against the chill yet needing to feel the sting of cold water against his face.

Five minutes later he spotted a lighted window far down the street and made for it. He was the restaurant's third customer. As he came in and sat at the plain pine counter, the sleepy-eyed waiter behind it suddenly came wide awake and answered his order for steak and eggs and coffee with a cordial, "Won't take a minute, stranger."

Sherill noticed that the waiter winked broadly at a pair of wide-hatted individuals further along the counter, noticed also that these two were eyeing him with some amusement and a quite open respect. He ignored all this and when his plate came he at once began wolfing down the food.

He had half-finished eating when the door opened and a cadaverously lean man entered. A gold shield was pinned to the buckle of the newcomer's shell-belt. He stopped just inside the door, looking kitchenward and calling, "Seen that wolfer yet, Hank?"

The restaurant man came through the curtain at the end of the counter, wiping his hands on his grimy apron. "Not yet, Marshal," he said.

"How about the other one?"

"Nope," Hank shook his head, his face a blank.

The marshal sighed tiredly, said, "Give a yell if you do," and went out onto the walk again. As his steps faded along the planking Hank's face broke into a wide grin and with a pointed look at Sherill, he returned to his kitchen.

Sherill was having his second cup of coffee when one of the 'punchers down the counter caught his eye and asked him, with a straight face, "See the fight last night?"

"Where?" Sherill asked blandly.

"At the *Fine and Dandy*."

"Was it any good?" Sherill queried.

The 'puncher nudged his neighbor. "Was it any good, he wants to know." He laughed. "Mister, the doc spent half the night settin' bones and sewin' cuts. That was the damnedest free for all I ever seen. They wrecked the place."

"I should've been there." Sherill smiled a little, then made a point of changing the subject, asking, "You with one of the outfits around here?"

"M on a Rail."

"Any range for lease out your way?"

"Not any."

The speaker's partner leaned over the counter now so that he could see Sherill, asking, "How much do you need, stranger?"

"Three or four sections anyway. Ten if I can get it."

"He could try Donovan, Bill."

"Who's Donovan?" Sherill wanted to know.

"Major Donovan. Bosses Anchor. Last winter a blow piled most of their stuff up against a drift fence. You can't see the fence for the bones. Stink, my God! Until a month ago, you couldn't ride that country."

Sherill was remembering Donovan now, thinking of Jean Ruick and what had happened last evening at the Sheriff's office. *Why not?* he finally asked himself. Then: "Where is this outfit?"

"Cross the river, take the road east and ride till you come to it. Two hours ought to get you there."

Sherill thanked them, paid for his breakfast and went on down to the *River House*. The lobby was deserted and dark except for a night lamp over the desk at the foot of the stairs. The door to the bar stood open and a clink of glasses sounded in there where a swamper was beginning to straighten up.

Upstairs Sherill found Ned Rawn sprawled across the bed still dressed in the gray suit, now badly rumpled. The window was closed and the air stale and heavy. Sherill threw up the window and momentarily considered waking his friend. But then he gave up the idea, remembering something of Ned's too-frequent mornings after.

He had come for his gun, Slim's .45, and now found it lying on the chair beside the wash stand. He pulled aside his jumper and thrust it through the waistband of his denims and presently, with a last glance toward the bed, he left the room.

Going along the hallway he glanced up into the blackness at its head, for a moment wondering about Ruth and then forcing himself not to think of the Lovelaces.

He remembered the big livery-lot he had passed as he came down the street with Jean Ruick yesterday afternoon, now guessing that it might be Kramer's. It was, a combination stage station, freight yard and livery. As he came up on it, a battered mud-wagon rolled out of the gate, laying a hollow thunder against the stillness as its two teams hit the plank ramp, the sound of its going at once muted by the street's heavy dust.

The night man hadn't heard about the saddle but remembered Sherill's geldings. So they went on back to the barn, found the saddle and Sherill watched the hostler rope one of the pair, a sorrel.

He rode on down to the levee and waded the river below the ferry landing in the first cold dawn light, his glance going to the *Queen* and clinging to it, unpleasantly interrupting his thoughts of Jean Ruick and his errand.

How long, he wondered, would it take him to know river boats and freight and bills of lading as well as he knew grass and leather and the good and bad points of a horse? *Years,* he told himself, for the first time really questioning his goal, this future the Commodore had forced on him last year during his visit to Hannibal.

The prospect wasn't pleasing and as he put the sorrel up the far bank and pushed on at a steady jog, he told himself, *One thing at a time,* and for the second time in this barely-begun day he forced his thoughts away from something that had to do with Ruth.

Caleb Donovan finished his breakfast in Anchor's cookhouse and left the table before the others. He went to the door and stood there idly working at his strong teeth with a quill toothpick, looking out across the creek willows to the hazed bulk of the far Sabers.

Presently, without turning, he said, "Better work that upper tank today, Phil," and Phil Rust, Anchor's straw-boss, replied, "We'll do that, Major." It wasn't long before Rust and the two others filed out past Donovan, heading for the wagonshed and corral.

He watched them hitch the team and load the scoop and presently take the trail to the south. He was irritable over this daily chore of having to think up enough work to keep three men busy where last spring there had been too much for six to handle, and now, hearing the cook clearing up in the room behind him, he dryly asked, "Brick, what did you put in those flapjacks this morning? Sand?"

He got no answer, hadn't expected any. He seemed to forget the toothpick, working it to the side of his mouth. Shortly he trudged across to the short office wing of the big log cabin, plainly not enjoying the walk. He was heavy without an ounce of fat on his bearlike frame, his two hundred and twenty pounds making him appear shorter than his five foot nine. His cavalryman's boots and close-fitting breeches were, in these surroundings, incongruous. But over the years he had flatly refused to break the habits of an Army upbringing and wear a high-heeled boot or sit anything but a McClellan saddle.

To heighten this appearance of individuality he wore his moustache close-clipped, unfashionably.

He was climbing the step to the office door when the sound of a trotting horse shuttled in across the draw. He came back down across the gravelled yard until he could see around the L-shaped cabin's corner. By that time a tall rider on a sorrel was already through the gate and climbing into the yard. Seeing him, the rider angled this way.

"Mornin'," Jim Sherill said as he came up. "I'm looking for Major Donovan."

"That's me."

Sherill came aground and they shook hands. Then, without preliminary, Sherill announced the reason for his visit, asking if there was any chance of leasing range.

Donovan's look brightened, although his tone was dry as dust when he said, "What do you think? You came along that fence."

Sherill nodded, feeling no little pity for the man. The sight of that half-mile long scattering of bones would have impressed any stockman. He wouldn't soon forget it.

"What's your offer?" Donovan asked.

"What's it worth?"

They began talking it over, Sherill not committing himself, Donovan fishing for an offer and occasionally reaching up and absentmindedly working the quill around his teeth. He was occupying himself in this fashion when he heard someone approaching beyond the corner of the cabin and turned in time to see Jean Ruick walk into sight half a dozen steps away.

She saw Sherill and stopped, surprise and a quick embarrassment touching her finely-moulded face. Sherill touched his hat to her and she nodded, on the verge of smiling, and hastily said, "I didn't know you were busy, Major."

She was turning away when Donovan stopped her. "Jean, this man's come out to ask about leasing those eight sections along the river. You ought to be in on it." He looked at Sherill, telling him, "Miss Ruick's the owner. You can talk to her."

Jean Ruick appeared reluctant to join them, asking, "Can't you decide it without me?"

"We can," Donovan said. "But it's a little out of the ordinary, Jean. Sort of hard to know a fair price to ask."

Sherill saw her hesitation and said, half-smiling, "Maybe you don't like it, Miss. But my money's printed by the same outfit that prints yours. And I'd pay in advance."

"Did I say I didn't like it?" There was a faint edge to her voice, although he could see that she was deliberately trying to keep

70

from showing him any animosity. She looked at Donovan now, telling him, "Major, this is the man who rode the mare into town yesterday."

"So?" Surprise was strong on Donovan's blocky face and he looked at Sherill oddly, in a wary way.

Sherill misunderstood both his word and his look and told the girl, "If I was here, you and the sheriff could both keep an eye on me." He let his smile broaden.

She started to smile, didn't, instead said carefully, "I've said nothing about wanting to watch you. If you and the Major can come to some agreement, that's between the two of you."

Sherill saw the pride that was in her, a pride that wouldn't let her openly admit yesterday's mistake although he sensed she was feeling differently about him today. He was struck by the thought, *She's damned handsome,* and was a little annoyed by it. He had been prepared not to like this girl. Yet the fact remained that her looks were quite striking just now, the early sunlight edging her head with spun copper and laying sharp highlights across her sensitive face. She was taller than he remembered, her rust-colored dress subtly revealing the graceful contours of her figure.

It was plain that the Major didn't want to decide this on his own, for now that he saw she was trying a second time to leave them he said, "He's offered two hundred for ninety days. I'm askin' three."

Jean Ruick looked at Sherill again, "Make it three hundred for four months."

"Ninety days is all I'd want it."

"Two hundred and fifty then."

"Two and a quarter's as high as I'd go."

"Take it, Major," she said.

Donovan nodded. "Sounds good all the way around. Unless you've got some reason for objectin', Jean."

"Let's say I had a reason," she said.

She gave Sherill one more measuring glance, then turned and disappeared around the wall-corner, and Donovan drawled, "She's calmed down considerable since last night. The mare barely made it out here tied to the back of her buckboard."

"The mare had taken a beating."

"Just what did happen?"

Sherill gave the Major the same story he'd given the sheriff and evidently satisfied his curiosity. They talked over the details of the lease, Sherill agreed to call at a lawyer's office in Whitewater to sign the agreement and they shook hands.

From the kitchen window, Jean watched

Sherill ride down and through the gate and go out the trail. Alter he had dipped out of sight beyond a far rise, she stood there a long moment, for the first time consciously realizing that she had made the effort to be nice to him. She couldn't analyze her contrariness, why it was that yesterday she had been so sure of one thing about him and today was equally as willing to be sure of the opposite.

But there it was, and because she was so completely honest with herself she admitted now that there were many things she liked about this Jim Sherill — that way he had of smiling with his eyes while his face remained grave, the look of his flat wide back tapering into narrow hips, and the strong sense of humor in him that yesterday in the sheriff's office had given her the impression he wasn't taking his threatened arrest a bit seriously.

Her curiosity about him was so strong that finally she turned from the window and left the kitchen, crossed the living room and went along the short bedroom hallway to the office.

She found Caleb Donovan at his desk writing a letter, the ever-present quill toothpick in the corner of his mouth. He looked up as she entered, leaned back in his chair and laid his pen aside.

"Jacobs over at Sands is offering ninety head of culls at twenty-five apiece, Jean," he said. "They're sound and average a hundred pounds under weight for the reservation herd. Do we buy?"

"Culls? Not at twenty-five, Major. Offer him twenty."

"And lose 'em? Jean, we've got an empty range. How do we get back in business?"

"By buying carefully." She let it go at that, knowing that the matter was settled. Lately the Major rarely pressed an argument with her.

She went to the room's far corner now and pushed a pair of saddlebags from the deep leather chair there, asking as she sat down, "Did Sherill take your offer?"

"Yours, you mean. Yes."

She smiled, musing, "I wonder."

"You wonder what?"

"How wrong I was about him yesterday."

He had no opinion to offer and sat waiting, knowing she had something more to say. At length her look changed to one of faint alarm. "He isn't using the bunkhouse, is he?"

"No. He wanted the shack on the river."

"Because of me, I suppose."

"He didn't say."

"He wouldn't." Her good humor held as she looked at Donovan. "You know, I don't for a minute think he knew he was riding a stolen horse."

"Probably not."

"Why don't you go on into town today and see what you can find out about him?"

He gave her an amused look. "Purely for business reasons, of course." She at once sobered and he laughed, saying, "All right. I was going in anyway to have Whipple draw up the papers. And as long as I'm that far I might as well go on up to Sands and look over those culls."

He wasn't looking at her and didn't see the quizzical glance she gave him as he went on, "I'll be back sometime tomorrow."

Over the next half hour, until the Major rode out the town trail, Jean tried to puzzle through the answer to his trip to Sands, not wanting to doubt him but unable to keep from it. He had been gone only ten minutes when finally, in desperation, she went to her room and took a letter from beneath the things in the bottom bureau drawer. Then she left the cabin, walking across to the cookhouse.

She found old Brick Chase scouring his counter at the range end of the long room. He looked up as she came in, said simply, "Hello, youngster," and went on with his work.

She sat on the end of one of the table benches, hardly knowing how to begin what she wanted to tell him.

In the end, he saved her that trouble. For his brief look at her had told him something. He had known her long enough — all of her twenty-three years — to be well acquainted with her moods. So now he asked, "Somethin' on your mind?"

"Yes, Brick." She sighed her relief. "Brick, sound underweight reservation culls are simply culls, aren't they?"

He turned, favoring his game leg, and drawled, "Sure thing. Why?"

"The Major is going over to Jacobs' place, at Sands, to look over ninety head of culls they're selling. He seemed to think he ought to see them before we buy."

Brick's bushy brows lifted but he didn't say anything. Studying his long and narrow face with its heavy moustache, graying in the same shade as his thinning carroty hair, Jean found enough assurance to go on, "We've never learned where he was during the blizzard last winter, have we?"

"Nope." The old cook's tone was strictly neutral.

She and Brick alone shared this secret. Last winter they had gone out into that storm together and cut fence on Brick's hunch that the cattle would drift that way during the blow. They'd been driven in finally by the fury of the storm and during that shrieking, bitter-cold night the cattle had hit the fence beyond the cuts and piled up there and died.

Jean had never forgiven the Major for leaving her alone with one lame man on the place, for being away himself during the blizzard.

It was Brick, driving the buckboard to Whitewater the same afternoon the Major returned, who discovered no tracks in the deep snow along the town trail. He hadn't mentioned it until days afterward, until it was too late for Jean to question her uncle's story of having waited out the blizzard in Whitewater. So she had filed away that item of information along with several others that were puzzling her, and neither she nor Brick had since spoken of it.

Now she took the long, official-looking envelope from the pocket of her dress, unfolded it and held it out to him, saying, "See what you think of this, Brick."

He wiped his hands on his flour-sacking apron before he took it, drew out the single sheet and read it.

Jean could remember every word of it.

Miss Jean Ruick
Whitewater, Montana
Dear Miss Ruick:
Regarding your recent inquiry, Caleb R.
Donovan, Captain, Cavalry, resigned his
commission 4 February, 1875. There is no
official record of any irregularity having ter-
minated this officer's career.

The letter was signed by the Adjutant General.

"So it's captain, not major," Brick drawled, limping over to hand the letter to her.

"That's just one more thing, Brick. I wish I knew more about him."

"But you don't."

"You hate him, don't you?" When he made no reply, she asked, "What would you do if you were me?"

"Get rid of him. He's damn' near ruined you, Jean!" For the first time, real emotion showed in the old man's face.

"How can I? He's Mother's brother. You know how she felt about him."

"She was afraid he couldn't look after himself. Your old man would never let him set foot on the place."

"Why, Brick?"

"John wasn't much given to talk. He never said."

"Dad must have known something about him that we don't."

"Maybe."

It helped to talk to Brick, who knew her better than any person alive. And she knew him well enough to appreciate that, although he willingly shared her confidences, he seldom pretended to give her advice. Even when she asked for it, he would let her reason things through for herself, now and then prodding her with his sparse-worded wisdom.

She knew that she couldn't do what he had suggested. She also knew that she couldn't change his mind, that it was up to her to come to some sort of a decision.

"How's he been treating you?" she asked.

"I look after myself."

She went to the door now, knowing only that she lacked any real facts upon which to base her suspicion of the Major.

She said, "We won't mention his really being a captain, Brick."

"Not on your life. From now on he's 'Colonel'."

"Don't you dare, Brick!"

He turned serious then, hobbling across to stand in the door as she stepped out. "I'd forget it, Jean. You got enough else to think about."

"You'd be the first one not to forget it,

Brick," she said as she left him.

Sherill reached the river at nine that morning and, crossing it, took a wetting to the knees when the sorrel struck a tricky stretch of quicksand and shied into deep water.

He wasn't sure that he could find his way in to the hideout from this point. But yesterday morning on the way out he had pretty accurately marked a low bald peak some ten miles north of the river, knowing he had passed it the previous night and that the trail he had ridden lay several miles east of it.

He spotted the peak now and, the river behind him, headed into a tangle of near-barren canyons and mesas and buttes. This torn and myriad-colored country lifted after some miles to the foothills and finally he was riding the timber, breathing the cool pine-scented air drifting off the peaks.

There was a subtle change in him now, an alertness that cocked his big frame further forward in the saddle, that made him unnaturally impatient at any lagging or misjudgment of the gelding's. His glance roved ahead restlessly and with a constant shifting from one bit of cover to another. Time and again he paused before crossing an open stretch of ground. If there was a way around it, he took it.

This was far different from his last ride into these hills. Then he had wanted them to find him. His chief worry had been to hide that fact, first of all by appearing genuinely surprised at meeting anyone, next to make a convincing yet unsuccessful attempt to get away. He had quite convinced Mitch and Slim, for they had appreciated how thoroughly beaten he was when they finally took him. Ed's strange suspicions had been something different, something he couldn't have anticipated. But, regardless of Ed, he had succeeded in keeping from them his identity as owner of the horses being worked in the big corral. That was the important thing.

There was another difference between this ride in and that first one. Then he had been simply trying to recover his horses. Now a great deal more was involved. His horse-herd had become the whole core of his future. To lose it would be to lose his hold on that future.

He was expecting anything and as another hour passed, then still another that put him abreast the granite shoulder of the bald peak, his vigilance strengthened rather than easing off. He had counted eight men up there at the hill ranch. Eight men could cover a lot of country in looking for him and Ed would see that they did.

He was fairly sure that they would still be hunting him. He had taken a lot of trouble to hide his sign on that hard night ride down through the hills that nearly killed the already jaded mare. Until Ed was sure of what had happened to him, he would reason that, hunted and riding a worn-out animal, his quarry would try and lose himself in this hill wilderness and not go beyond the river until he was in better shape to travel.

Sherill was sure of one more thing in the light of Ed's suspicions. That crew would be riding with orders to shoot him on sight.

So as he struck east from the peak, now following a high line through the aspen, he made several detours that took him around low-lying and open ground. He was going generally east, knowing that if he was careful and had average luck he could spot the trail. It would lead him up to the long meadow and he was going to try to come in on the layout from the timber to the north.

Finally the trail came into sight far below as he was taking a chance he knew he shouldn't. He had left the timber to ride to the edge of a high rim and inspect the country below it. The risk he ran in briefly sky-lining himself consequently paid off. But as he went on he was nervous about it.

He rode north now, paralleling the trail.

Shortly a higher barrier of rimrock drove him down into the lower country. On the way down there were long stretches of open ground. He crossed these as fast as he could, sometimes punishing the sorrel with the spur in his urgency to stay out of sight.

He was no sooner in the timber of these lower hills than, rounding the wall of the rim that had blocked him, this depression narrowed and ran along a canyon. Abruptly he came to a stretch where the tall lodgepole pines thinned, giving him no choice but to cross four hundred yards of the open canyon bed to gain the shelter of the timber above.

He held the sorrel to a fast trot all the way across, his nerves tight-strung and his glance warily studying what lay ahead. He was entering that upper stand of timber, the tension in him easing away, when the gelding suddenly lifted his head and whickered, looking off to the right. Then a voice shuttled down out of the trees off there, sharply saying:

"Not so fast!"

III

Mitch Lockwood saw Sherill's head come around, saw him weigh his chances and at once discard them; all this in an instant.

A vast relief flowed through Mitch. Since sighting Sherill on that high rim twenty minutes ago, he had known that he wasn't going to use the Winchester on the stranger as certainly as he had known that this carefully planned interception would bring them together.

Now his thought was, *Ed won't take this from me.* He lifted the carbine's barrel a trifle in a gesture Sherill immediately understood. He leaned there, elbows on the top of the outcrop, the Winchester still held ready, and watched Sherill carefully pull his jumper aside and lift out the Colt's and toss it to the ground.

He straightened then and stepped back to gather up the reins of his ground-haltered roan. He led the horse on down through the trees and picked up Sherill's gun. Giving Sherill a steady glance, he drawled:

"Some people never learn. You must be one of 'em."

Sherill's slow grin came then and Mitch's thought was, *Does anything bother him?* as Sherill asked, "Why didn't you let me have it?"

"Because I got you into this," Mitch said angrily. "Because I think Ed made a wrong guess. And may be because I think you need lookin' after."

"I get along all right," Sherill drawled.

Mitch ignored the remark, tilting his head. "The trail's off there over that hill. Hit it and follow it out. Clear out. And don't come back. The bunch is workin' that country west of here today. You won't be stopped."

"I've already been out."

Mitch noticed Sherill's wide hat now, drawling, "So I see. Well, you're goin' again. For good."

"Not before I've seen Ed."

Strong surprise momentarily widened Mitch's eyes. He saw where he had been wrong about something. "So you weren't lost after all," he said. He caught Sherill's shake of the head and asked impatiently, "Why see Ed?"

"We might help each other along."

Mitch smiled coldly. "Ed Stedman ever help anyone?"

"He'll listen to me."

"Look," Mitch said with a thin patience,

"Ed's ribs may be caved in from the lamp you tossed at him. He's not sure yet. And Slim's got a hole through his leg and a busted face you gave him."

"Ed'll still listen."

Mitch gave Sherill a long and completely baffled inspection. Finally he sighed wearily and, turning away, said, "I can think of fancier ways of dyin'. But we all got our own ideas." He thrust the carbine in its scabbard and climbed up into leather.

"So you'll take me in?"

"Can I keep you out?" Mitch asked angrily. "You know the way now."

Sherill held out a hand. "Then how about my iron?"

"Now I know you're loco. Hunh-uh! I like to know how I stand around a wild man." Mitch nodded toward the higher trees. "You first."

Sherill led the way on up through the pines and around the tangles of scrub-oak and presently, over that low rise, they came to the trail that footed the canyon's east wall.

There was no stir of air and the heat was trapped in this narrow corridor and as they turned up along the trail Sherill shrugged out of his jumper and laid it across his thighs behind the horn of the saddle.

Farther on, where the canyon broadened and the trail lifted obliquely across open ground, he drew in on the sorrel and let Mitch come up on him, drawling, "So Ed's not feeling too good?"

Mitch came abreast, to Sherill's right and not close. "So sore he can't stand straight."

Sherill laughed softly. "It's a good thing the lamp went out." He idly rested his free hand on his thigh, on the jumper.

"We thought of that, too," was Mitch's dry comment.

Sherill's right arm arced out suddenly, swinging the jumper by the neckband as he kneed the sorrel in at Mitch. The bottom of the jumper caught Mitch across the face an instant after he saw what was coming. He dropped his hand to his gun.

Sherill rolled out of the saddle and dove at him, catching his lifting right arm as their animals shied apart. Sherill's weight dragged Mitch off balance and they both fell, Mitch underneath when they hit the ground. A moment later the Colt's spun from his hand.

Mitch was quick and tough, cunning at this rough and tumble sort of a fight. Before Sherill knew it, he had squirmed from under him and they were simultaneously coming to their feet.

Mitch hit Sherill above the heart in a vicious

quick punch. But he didn't follow through and was too slow lifting his guard and Sherill threw a fast jab with a lot of weight behind it that raked him across the mouth. He tried to close on Sherill and couldn't. He knew then that he was fighting a faster man.

⌐ He was a little groggy and the salty taste of blood was in his mouth. He kept doggedly lunging in and not finding Sherill, seeing him plainly enough but somehow not hitting him. He took two more solid blows in the face and then some more and the last ones he didn't feel at all. He didn't know he was down until his sight cleared and he found himself lying on his back looking up at Sherill's tall shape.

Sherill wore Mitch's belt and holster now. The handle of his own Colt's stuck out above the belt of his waist-overalls. He looked down at Mitch and gravely asked, "Why didn't you quit?"

Mitch tried to hate him and couldn't, his instinct of liking the man too strong to be crowded out. But he did hate being licked this way after landing only one solid punch. So now, without answering, he rolled over and pushed up onto his knees, thinking as slowly as he moved, *This finishes me with Ed.* He stayed on his knees for several seconds, head hung and waiting for the ground to stop spinning beneath him. He felt blood dripping from his chin and didn't care.

He got to his feet finally. He lunged in at Sherill with what he thought was quickness.

Sherill lazily sidestepped him, then caught him as he was falling. Sherill pinned his arms before he could swing, drawling, "Quit, will you!" and Mitch swung a boot back and raked Sherill across the shin with the blunt star-rowel of a spur.

Mitch felt Sherill's hold suddenly tighten and the sky tilted at a crazy angle and then he was being thrown to the ground hard. His head snapped back and struck something solid. For a split-second he was fighting to keep his senses.

That second interval of total blackness was much longer than the first and Mitch came out of it gradually this time, at first aware only of his head wanting to split open with its aching and of his head swaying so that he couldn't control it. Then over his torment he vaguely recognized the feel of the saddle under him and knew that he was on a horse and that the horse was moving.

Finally he dared to open his eyes and it was hard to see through the pinkish haze and pick up blurred images coming toward him and then sliding past. He felt a tightness in his arms and tried to lift them and couldn't.

The motion of the horse stopped suddenly and he could indistinctly hear voices over the singing in his head. He looked down and for the first time really understood what he was seeing.

His shell-belt was around his waist, pinning his arms to his sides at the elbows. He lifted his eyes and even in this semi-conscious condition could hardly believe what he saw.

There was Ed's small cabin and the bunk-house and the high bulk of the sideless barn in the background through the pines. *An hour,* he thought, *I've been out for an hour, anyway.*

Then alongside him Sherill was saying, "Would I have brought him on in if I didn't want to be here?"

Mitch moved his head around and saw Sherill beside him, holding him erect by a grip on one arm. Then, beyond Sherill, he saw Ed Stedman standing a few feet away holding the Greener, the shotgun's twin bores tilted up at Sherill. His carbine and the two Colt's, his and Sherill's, lay there in the dust near Ed.

He mumbled, "Couldn't help it, Ed," but the words didn't seem to make sense and if Ed heard he gave no sign of it.

Ed said now, "Let go of him and get down. Slow."

"He'll fall," Sherill told him.

"Let him fall," Ed said.

Sherill let go of his arm and as a matter of pride, to spite Ed, Mitch managed to hold himself upright in the saddle.

He watched Ed motion with the shotgun, watched Sherill step on past Ed. And then the two of them were heading up to the cabin.

Wearily, Mitch lifted his hands and worked the buckle of the belt around to his front and finally loosened it. He was oddly worried about Sherill, more worried about him than about himself. But there was nothing he could do now to help the man.

He let his weight go forward against the horn, took a tight grip on it and slid to the ground. He kept holding onto the horn, mumbling, "Whoa, fella, whoa!" to the horse until he was sure his legs would take his weight.

Finally he pushed away from the roan and stumbled across to the bunkhouse. It took a lot of his strength to step up and through the door. He looked dazedly across the long room with its double row of bunks, the stove at the center and the table at this near end.

He saw Slim lying asleep in the bunk under the window, the leg of his overalls rolled to the knee showing his bandaged calf. He walked over there and stood looking down at Slim's bruised face, swaying a little.

There was something he wanted to tell Slim. But he couldn't make his voice work. So instead he told himself what he had on his mind. *He's tough. As tough as they come. So don't feel so damned sorry for yourself.*

He walked over to his own bunk then and let his weight collapse onto it. He closed his eyes, feeling a deep peace settle through him, no longer thinking of Sherill or of anything except to wonder how long he'd be out this time.

Across in the small cabin, the shotgun lay across the desk pointing at Sherill. Ed Stedman's hand rested idly beside it. Sherill wasn't much given to talk but he was talking now, trying to beat back the cold reserve that kept Ed's face and pale eyes a blank.

"If I'm a Canadian, why don't I talk like one?" he asked. "No, I was in trouble up there and had to get out in a hurry. I took the first horse I saw, then swapped him for your blue."

Ed said nothing but kept staring at him in that enigmatic way, sitting hunched over a little from his sore chest. Sherill was beginning to think he couldn't make his story stick, that he'd have to get out of here. The door was behind him, open, maybe two strides away. *Too far,* he decided, and knew that he had no choice now but to keep on talking, playing for a break.

He said patiently, "I had that forty-four of Lockwood's just now. If it was you I was after, I'd have tied Lockwood onto his hull and sent that horse on in ahead of me. Then I could've picked you off when you came out to look at him."

"What is it you're after?" Ed asked, speaking for the first time in all these minutes.

"I want to make a deal with you," Sherill said.

A meager smile touched Ed's gaunt face. "I make the deals. If there are any. If."

Sherill asked bluntly, "How often do you work this many horses through here?"

"Who said they were goin' through?"

"All right, I'll put it another way. If," and Sherill emphasized that word, "you had a crew that thought the way you did, and *if* you wanted to pick up horses on the quiet, work their brands and sell 'em, you've got the right kind of a layout."

"Somebody said that once," Ed drawled.

Sherill played the game, soberly saying, "Last night down in Whitewater I got to thinking about it and — "

"Whitewater?" Ed cut in, showing the faintest trace of surprise.

"I told you the other night I was going there. I did. I know a man there."

"Who?"

"Man by the name of Rawn. Ned Rawn."

"The remount buyer?"

"Yes. We can use him in this."

"In what?" Ed's tone was still neutral.

"In swapping these horses," Sherill told him.

Ed asked, tonelessly, "Who said we were swappin' any horses?"

Sherill saw that he had to do something to break down the man's suspicion. He acted instinctively then, shrugging and saying, "All right, I can always go to someone else."

"You can if I let you," Ed said smoothly, his lips hardly moving. "Go on with what you started to say."

"Down in Whitewater I asked a few questions. No one seemed to know about many jugheads disappearin' from that country down there. Why is it, I asked myself. This is the sweetest layout I ever came across. Hard to find. Set so you could work horses in from both ends. From as far south as Wyoming and as far north as Canada. You could work the brands, then get rid of your Wyoming horses up north and the Canadian ones in the south."

"We don't fool much with Canadian horses," Ed said.

94

Now he's opening up was Sherill's thought as he went on, "Then you're missing a good bet. Another thing. Rawn knows me well enough so he'd work in any stuff we had that was good enough for the Army. Geldings, all solid colors, fifteen to sixteen hands. He'd pay eighty apiece."

Ed reached over now and deliberately moved the Greener aside. He leaned forward and picked up a sack of tobacco.

As he built his smoke, he said, "I could always get along with a man that had something between the ears. Help yourself to a chair."

Jake Henry had stirred several times that morning and had kept his eyes closed against the pulsing throb of his head, each time dropping off to sleep again. But by eleven the heat of the loft was close to unbearable and he was feeling a little better. At last he sat up, for a time holding his head in his hands.

Finally, he noticed his torn sleeve and took off the jacket. He repaired the tear with several strips of the sleeve's leather fringe, all the while thinking back on the fight last night and remembering enough of it to know that they would probably be looking for him today. Getting his mule out of Kramer's corral would be no cinch.

He also remembered what Sherill had told him last night and was more than a little worried about Sherill's predicament. Now he made his guess on where Sherill must have gone today and the urgency to get back up into the hills was all at once strong in him.

He had taken chances all his life and he took one now, believing in his luck. He climbed brazenly down out of the loft and was out of the barn and climbing through the poles of the corral before the hostler became curious enough to come to the feed-room door to see who had walked through the barn. By that time Jake was out of sight along the alley.

He reached Kramer's by a devious back-street route and entered the corral at the back. No one was around and he caught his mule and, with a halter on her, led her over to the leanto behind the barn. Just then a roustabout who was cleaning out the stalls saw him lugging his saddle from the leanto. The youngster laid his pitchfork aside and, glancing back over his shoulder, was on the way up to tell the others when Jake called to him:

"Bub, get back here and give me a hand."

The boy's awe of Jake decided the matter of whether he should run or do as he was told. Reluctantly, he came out of the barn and, staring at Jake wide-eyed, helped saddle the mule.

Jake paid him and asked him to open the back gate. For a few seconds it looked as though the youngster was going to panic and make a run for it, seeing Jake getting away so easily. But he was afraid of the wolfer. So he walked on back and opened the gate. Afterwards, as Jake went up the alley, the boy ran shouting across the corral. By the time the word got around, Jake was well out of town and running his mule hard along the steep grade of the bluff road.

Caleb Donovan was leaving the sheriff's office at about the time Jake was making good his getaway. Donovan had learned little more than Jean and Sherill had already told him, except that Fred Spence wasn't liking it much that Sherill hadn't stopped in at the jail this morning before leaving town.

Donovan couldn't locate Ned Rawn and so set about his errands, a call at his lawyer's office, a trip to the feed store and then to the bank. He ate his midday meal early and afterward, with the ever-present quill toothpick in the corner of his mouth, he went along to the post-office and mailed a postcard to Jacobs, in Sands, offering twenty dollars a head for the culls.

He needed a shave and turned in at the barber-shop. The barber was stropping his razor, Donovan lying back with a hot towel on his face, when the man in the next chair said, "They tell me there's a high stake game on in Bill Meadows' back room. Been goin' since yesterday morning."

Donovan filed away this piece of information and later he followed his hunch and went on up the street to Meadows' hardware store.

He found Ned Rawn at the table in the room behind the office. Rawn's thin face was pale and showing strain. They asked Donovan into the game and he answered that he might be back later. Then he asked to speak to Rawn privately and he and Rawn went on back through the storeroom to the loading platform at the rear.

"Hate to drag you out of there, Rawn," Donovan said in the careful manner he affected with men he didn't know well.

"Forget it," Ned said in his genial way, "just so long as you don't want to borrow money. They've got all mine."

"Stick with it and your luck always changes," Donovan told him, continuing, "What I wanted to ask about was Sherill."

"What about him?"

"He'd like to lease part of our range."

"Well?"

Donovan fiddled with his teeth a moment, staring obliquely at Ned. "Will I get my money?"

Ned's face tightened a little. "Why wouldn't you?"

"Well, he was riding that stolen mare yesterday."

"He explained that."

"Then so far as you know he's honest?"

"Not only honest, he's the best damned man I've ever known. Any way you look at it. Does that suit you, Major?"

Donovan smiled, hoping he hadn't offended. "It certainly does. Much obliged. By the way, where's he from?"

"Down in my country." Ned took out his watch, looked at it and bluntly said, "I've got to be going."

He turned then without a further word and went back into the store and Donovan stood staring at the empty doorway feeling let-down and disgusted with himself. He'd only started on the questions he really wanted to ask about Sherill. Now he knew he had gone about it the wrong way.

Some ten minutes later, on his way up the street after his horse, he was still feeling that disgust. This was the reason for his scowl when, on hearing someone behind him call his name, he stopped and turned.

He saw George Lovelace walking up to him and gave a start of surprise. A momentary guarded expression masked his features. Then, in answer to Lovelace's broad smile, his face took on a forced look of geniality.

"Lord, you're the last person I'd expect to run into, Captain," Lovelace said cordially, extending his hand. "It's been all of six or seven years, hasn't it?"

"At least seven," Donovan said as they shook hands. "You're still the same, Commodore. Not a day older."

Lovelace chuckled. "Fightin' this river doesn't give a man time to grow old." His face went sober as he asked, "Located around here, Captain?"

Donovan nodded. "Helping my niece run a ranch."

"That's fine, just fine," Lovelace said. Then he gravely added, "It was unfortunate, your quitting the Army. Most unfortunate. But I suppose now you're glad you're out of it."

"It's the best thing that ever happened to me," Donovan said. He was feeling uncomfortable for the second time in the past quarter-hour and now, remembering how Rawn had left him, he took out his watch and looked at it, saying, "Sorry, Commodore, but I'm already late meeting a man. Where you staying? My next time in, we'll have a drink together."

"We certainly will," Lovelace answered. "You can always find me down at the *River House.*"

They shook hands again and Lovelace was his usual over-cordial self as they parted.

The Major lost no time in leaving town. He took the road in the opposite direction from Sands. If he was disappointed at the outcome of his meeting with Ned Rawn, he was more than disappointed in having come across Lovelace.

On leaving Donovan, Ned Rawn didn't go back to the poker game but headed for the street. *Six thousand,* he said to himself, *and last week it was four.* He was careful to think no further back than that and now his bony face was tight-drawn and pale, a mirror of his dismal ponderings.

Easy money had worked more of a change in Ned than even Jim Sherill had suspected. Sherill was well acquainted with his friend's strong instinct for gambling. But he didn't know that Ned's appetite for taking chances with money had increased since that original gamble when Ned had sunk every cent he could lay hands on into horses and brought them up here to fill his first contract with the Army.

It was typical of Ned that he had bought his way into the remount business by bribing an Army vet to overlook the questionable soundness of certain of his horses. It was also typical of his shrewdness that he had never since offered another bribe.

Ned was easy-going and downright likeable and Whitewater thought of him as an amiable and well-to-do bachelor, perhaps a little over-fastidious in his dress. Ramsay, the remount officer at Fort Selby, was his good friend because he never hesitated to do the Army a good turn, such as putting them onto good buys in feed. With the town and the Army so solidly behind him, Ned could have saved his money and actually become what they believed him to be, modestly well off. Instead, the ups and downs of cards had kept him either on the verge of going broke or with so much money that he could dream of amassing a real fortune.

Today that dream was hazy beyond the curtain of his disappointment over these recent losses. He was wondering now which of his friends was good for a loan, knowing he was limited in his borrowing to the tight circle of the poker crowd, all of whom were close-mouthed.

Bill Meadows, he decided, would be good

for a thousand. He wouldn't borrow beyond that unless forced to and now, seeing a possible way out of this tight corner, he immediately felt better.

He had slept only four hours last night and he needed food and a drink and there was no hurry about getting back to the game. So he headed downstreet for the *River House*, his spirits rising to the point where he started whistling in rhythm with his long stride.

He called for whiskey at the bar and was pouring his second drink when George Lovelace looked in from the lobby, spotted him and came across, saying affably, "You've been keeping out of sight, Ned. Let me buy this one."

"My turn, Commodore." Ned nodded to the apron to bring another glass, and when it came he offered Lovelace the bottle.

Lovelace poured and they drank and only after they had set their glasses down did the Commodore ask, "Have you seen Sherill?"

"No. Never expect Jim till you see him."

The Commodore let an expression of deep solemnity come to his face. "You know, Ned, Sherill and I had some pretty strong words last night."

Ned frowned. "What's the matter?"

"It's those horses. He won't call in help and I think he should."

103

"Don't worry, Commodore. Jim'll make out all right."

"But suppose he doesn't?" Lovelace asked.

"But he will, Commodore. If it'll ease your mind any, he's so sure of it that he's leased range to hold the horses on until time for the next delivery."

"You don't say!"

Ned nodded. "Caleb Donovan, who runs an outfit east of here, told me about it less than fifteen minutes ago."

He noticed the surprise that came to Lovelace's face but couldn't understand it. Lovelace was about to mention knowing Donovan when some instinct in him worked against it. So, to cover his surprise, he insisted, "Suppose all this doesn't work out for Jim?"

"He can stand the loss."

"Maybe he can," Lovelace said. "But what about Ruth? I can't let her marry a poor man. She couldn't stick it with him. Why, Ned, when that girl wants a dress she takes the boat up to St. Louis and comes back with a dozen. She's always got six or eight darkies around to look after her. She even brought one on this trip. Spoiled rotten, she is, and it's my fault. But I spoiled her mother the same way and was never sorry. Gave her everything she ever wanted. Nothing was too good for her."

Ned said deliberately, "You're right, Commodore. A beautiful woman should have everything."

George Lovelace's seriousness didn't melt before this gallantry. "What's Sherill got to offer her if he loses those horses?"

"Not much," Ned admitted.

"Now if it was you, I wouldn't spend a minute's thought on it," Lovelace said in an off-hand way. "You've got yours salted away. Sherill hasn't."

Ned was flattered. He covered his slight confusion by saying loyally, "Don't give up hope on Jim, Commodore. He has a way of doing what he sets out to do."

"I know. Damn it, I've told more people what a fine man he is. People down around the plantation. Now if I bring Ruth home without him they're going to be asking questions."

"Chances are you'll be taking Jim along."

"Think so?" The Commodore's look brightened considerably. "Well, here's hoping."

They refilled their glasses and drank again and then Lovelace looked up at Ned to say, "I've been thinking of something. There's a lot of people around this town who've been mighty nice to me. Before I go, I want to have them all down to the boat for some real southern cooking."

"Count me in on that, Commodore."

"I certainly will, my boy. Fact is, I'd thought of having the party tomorrow night. The judge is leaving on a trip the day after and I'd want him to be there. How would tomorrow suit you?"

"Fine. You couldn't keep me away."

The Commodore was sober now. "Suppose Jim hasn't shown up by then? Would you look after Ruth? You're her best friend here."

"I'd be honored, Commodore."

"Then let's count on it." The matter was settled. Lovelace offered the bottle to Ned, saying, "This one's mine," and they filled their glasses once more.

They had that drink and talked of several commonplace things and the Commodore finally made his excuses and left. He went straight upstairs, remembering Ned's mention of Caleb Donovan in a calculating way, thinking back on what he knew of the man.

His knock at Ruth's door was answered by Lou, Ruth's colored girl. There was a moment's delay and then Ruth told him to come in.

He found her getting ready for a bath, Lou about to fill a large zinc tub with pails of water she had carried up from the kitchen.

Ruth sat before the dresser mirror, wearing nothing but a light cotton wrapper and pinning her pale gold hair high on her head.

"Get on out, Lou," Lovelace said in his lordly way. And, when she had gone, "Daughter, where's your modesty? Cover up your front."

"Don't be cranky, Dad. After all, I wasn't expecting an audience."

Ruth nevertheless adjusted the wrapper so that it no longer exposed the creamy white skin above her small breasts. Then she got up to take her clothes from the room's only other chair.

George Lovelace's glance followed her affectionately and somewhat proudly. The wrapper revealed her figure in a way the fashionable full-skirted dresses never did and he was inclined to agree with Ned Rawn that she was a beautiful woman.

Taking the chair, he said casually, "Saw Ned downstairs just now. He's certainly a fine looking man."

"Has he seen Jim?"

"No," Lovelace cleared his throat, trying to keep the impatience out of his voice. Then, seeing that Ruth was watching him in the mirror as she did her hair, he brightened considerably.

"Ruth, I had an idea and talked it over

with Ned," he went on. "How would you like to help me entertain some of my friends on the boat tomorrow night? If Jim isn't back, Ned could take you. In fact, he asked if he could."

Ruth's hands slowly came down and she just as slowly turned to look at him. For long seconds her regard was steady, probing, and gradually her pretty face took on a knowing smile. "So you've thrown Jim over," she said.

"Now look here, Ruth! I — "

Her shake of the head cut him off. "Don't bother explaining. It's all right with me." She stared beyond him wistfully adding, "It'll have to be all right, won't it?"

"Damn it, girl! You're imagining things. Jim may even be here. He — "

"You could wait until you're sure he'll be here."

Lovelace's round face took on a ruddier tinge. "We can't wait forever. I've got obligations to these people. Suppose the river rises and we have to leave?"

"Yes, Dad. Of course."

Over a short silence he asked gruffly, "Anything the matter with Ned Rawn?"

"Nothing. But it would have been nice to dance once more with Jim."

"All right. We'll wait," he said stubbornly.

She shook her head, turning back to the mirror. "No, Dad. We won't wait. Jim had his chance and lost it. Ned's quite a catch and we can't miss this opportunity."

"What the devil are you saying?" he asked indignantly.

"Only what we're both thinking. Ned has money. Quite a lot probably. But does he know that the *Princess* caught fire and burned with her cargo the week after we left? Does he know that you were rained out of a crop of cotton? That you can barely meet your payroll?"

"God in Heaven, woman!" he shouted. "Why should he?"

"Sh-h-h!" she whispered mockingly. "Lou might hear." She turned a steady eye on him now and, half-smiling, said, "Don't worry, Dad. I'll not give you away. After all, I'm as anxious as you are to . . . How shall I put it? To make a suitable match?"

By three o'clock that afternoon Jean had finished most of the things that needed doing about the cabin and was standing at the porch door, looking out across the clean-raken yard and the garden with the white picket fence beyond it. She was thinking that this was the most pleasant place she had ever seen. *But lonely, too,* she told herself.

109

This was the beginning of her second summer here without her father, alone, and lately she had been restless and perhaps less interested in keeping up the house than usual. She often thought of her father and of their short time together, just that one year after her return from the academy in Illinois where she had gone to school and then stayed on to teach two more years. And today she had several times wondered what John Ruick would be doing if he could be in her present situation.

She felt she had dealt with Sherill quite fairly. Her mistake about the mare last evening had been a natural one and this morning she had made a few concessions to try and correct it. Sherill could be watched, although she doubted that he needed watching.

The Major posed an entirely different problem. It was in dealing with him that she would have liked to fall back on her father's sure judgment and iron hand.

Now she forced this unpleasant turn of mind into the background, wondering if she should bake a cake and take it down to Brick for the crew's supper. She went into the kitchen and had opened the flour-bin when her glance happened to go out the window to the rolling horizon and the distant twin ribbons of the road to the north. A boil of dust showed far out there.

A thought struck her sharply and she dropped the sifter back into the bin and went to the door, calling, "Brick!"

She saw him come to the cookhouse door and called, "Will you saddle the claybank?"

She ran to her room then and changed into her gray riding habit. Brick was leading the claybank up to the porch as she came down the steps.

"Goin' somewhere, youngster?" he asked.

"Just out to get the mail." She let him help her up to the side-saddle, hooking her leg around its projection and then adjusting her skirt.

"Early for the stage, ain't it?" Brick asked.

"No. It just came over the ridge."

She looked down at him, smiling at the curiosity he was taking some pains to hide. She seldom got mail these days and she knew he knew it. So she said mischievously, "Maybe there's a new driver, Brick," and wheeled the claybank away and ran across the yard before he had figured out what she meant.

It was a little over two miles out to the road and she ran the claybank all the way, not wanting to miss the stage. When she reached the junction of trail and road it was lifting over the crest of a hill a quarter-mile away and soon she could hear the rumble of its coming.

The driver saw her and pulled in on his three teams, a fog of dust overtaking the coach. Two passengers looked out as the high-bodied Concord lurched to a stop beside her, rocking gently on its thoroughbraces, and the old driver called down, "No luck today, Jean."

"Wasn't expecting anything really, Ben," she said, smiling up at him. "But I can always hope."

He laughed, glad for this break in his long run, thinking that John Ruick's daughter got better looking every time he saw her, which wasn't often enough.

"How's the Major?" he asked now, purely out of courtesy.

"Just the same," she told him. Then: "Would you do something for me, Ben?"

"Be glad to."

"I'm out of hairpins," she said quite seriously. "Could you bring me out two packages tomorrow? Those bone ones, not the big size. Brown, if they have them. I'll be waiting here for you."

Ben's weathered face reddened. He lifted a hand and with the back of it uneasily stroked his longhorn moustache, stammering, "Well now . . . you mean I got to . . .

Heck, I'd like to help you out, Jean, but . . ."

She could no longer keep a straight face and suddenly burst out laughing. One of the passengers joined in with a loud guffawing and Ben, his face beet-red, tried to say something and couldn't make himself heard.

Finally, with a sheepish grin, he kicked off his brake and swung his whip so that it exploded between the ears of the off-leader. The horses lunged against the traces and the Concord swayed and rolled away.

The stage was dipping out of sight along a downgrade four hundred yards away when Ben turned and waved with his hat. Jean lifted a hand and answered, breathless from her laughing.

Then she remembered her real reason for coming out here and a deep gravity rode over the brightness of her face. She had wanted information from Ben and he had given it to her by inquiring about the Major. Ben's run had today brought him from Sands to Whitewater and now was taking him on to Gap. He had come off the Sands road an hour and a half ago. Had he seen the Major, he would have mentioned it rather than asking about him.

So he didn't go to Sands was her thought as the worry about Donovan came crowding back again.

★ ★ ★

Up in the hill cabin, Sherill and Ed Stedman had talked for the better part of half an hour. Ed's manner had changed considerably since that moment when he had reached over to move the shotgun so that it wasn't pointing in Sherill's direction. He had become genial, at times almost enthusiastic over what Sherill had said.

But now Sherill had put the final question, "When do we start?" and the silence hung heavy and unbroken as he waited for Ed's answer.

Outside, the scolding voice of a jay rode the quiet and from the front of the cabin came the muffled stomping of the sorrel and Mitch's roan against the annoyance of the flies.

Ed said finally, "Give me a day or two."

"Why? Because you're still not sure about me?"

In answer, Ed reached down to a drawer of the desk and lifted out the shell-belt and the holstered horn-handled Colt's Sherill had left up here night before last. "Maybe this'll prove something." He pushed the weapon across the desk.

Sherill eyed first the gun and then the man. He shook his head, not reaching for the gun. "How does it? Just because you

114

let me leave here? Hell, if I'd wanted to ride for my health, I could have picked an easier spot to go to."

Ed smiled thinly, nothing more.

"We can't lose on this," Sherill insisted. "All you need is a place up north somewhere below the line. You work the two layouts, this one and the one north, along with that range I've leased. I feed you as much as you can handle, first from Wyoming. I'll bring these horses through fast and from far away so the local tin stars won't bother us. What could go wrong with that?"

"Cool down, man," Ed said with a low laugh. "I'm all for it. It sounds good. But I'd like to think it over."

Talk it over, you mean. The thought struck Sherill suddenly, and now he knew he must have hit on the only answer to Ed's strange reluctance to decide this matter here and now. Ed wasn't able to decide for himself.

Sherill reached for the belt now and stood up and buckled it on. "When do you want me back here?"

"Tomorrow or the day after. Or stay right here. Suit yourself." Ed came up out of his chair, drawling, "Damned if I thought I'd ever get together with you on anything."

"Want to call it off?"

"No. It sounds good."

"But you've got to think it over," Sherill said dryly.

Ed simply shrugged and, knowing nothing more could be done about this, Sherill turned and led the way outside.

As they passed the roan and came up on the sorrel, Ed said, "Mitch has been kinda red-headed about losin' his saddle the other night. Come on. I'll show you where yours is."

Sherill, reaching for the sorrel's reins, thought of something that made him drawl, "If this thing goes through, you've got to keep Lockwood out of my hair."

"I'll have a talk with Mitch."

"I mean that. Either he takes the chip off his shoulder or one of us gets hurt."

"He'll quit fightin' the bit," Ed said. "He knew what he was supposed to do and he wasn't takin' any chances with you."

They walked on past the bunkhouse, Sherill leading the gelding and saying, "He's a wild man. Wouldn't listen to a thing I had to say."

"Good. Now I'll know I can count on him."

They changed saddles, Sherill noting that his blanket roll hadn't been touched. He left shortly, heading for the creek and the trail beyond it, and Ed stood watching until he rode out of sight into the lower timber. Then Ed went back to his office, too preoccupied to notice that the roan no longer stood in the yard.

Five minutes ago Mitch had wakened to the sound of voices close to the bunkhouse, instantly recognizing them. He had gone to the window to see Ed and Sherill, leading the sorrel, walking off through the trees in the direction of the barn.

Sight of Sherill roused a rankling humiliation in him over the beating he had taken. As he stepped out to the washstand alongside the door and rinsed the dried blood from his bruised and swollen face, he was trying to remember just where he had made his mistake in that fight. The more he thought about it, the madder it made him.

When he next looked off toward the barn it was to see Sherill astride the sorrel heading down toward the trail. A sudden and unreasoning fury hit him as he understood that this big stranger had reached some sort of an agreement with Ed. Not caring what it was, he knew only that Sherill had been sure of himself the whole day, too sure. Just now he saw a certain arrogance even in the way Sherill sat the saddle, erect and with a certain lazy grace.

Just then he noticed his still-saddled roan

117

standing there. The next moment he was obeying an impulse too strong to turn aside. He ran for the roan and climbed into leather and walked the horse into the trees west of the trail. Beyond the creek, he kicked the animal to a hard run.

The pines thinned out half a mile below the meadow, and by some hard riding Mitch managed to hit the trail below Sherill where the timber ringed a deep basin. He pulled in and looked back up the trail and saw Sherill before it even occurred to him that he wasn't carrying his Colt's.

But a weapon had no place in his calculations and, stubbornly now, he swung aground and walked a dozen paces up the trail. He was waiting there as Sherill rode in on him.

"You again," Sherill drawled, reining in.

"Get down." Mitch's voice was brittle with anger.

"Why should I?"

"To see how good you really are," Mitch said tonelessly. "Hang that iron where you can't reach it and get on your feet."

Sherill could easily have ridden around him and out of here and Mitch knew it. But he had sampled this big man's stubbornness and was counting on it now. He was therefore unsurprised when Sherill presently took off the belt, hung it from the horn and swung aground.

Sherill drawled, "You're a bull-headed devil," as he stepped away from the gelding.

He was barely three strides away and Mitch at once drove in and swung at him. He turned sideways, taking the blow on his shoulder, not even lifting his hands. Mitch hit him again, this time a glancing blow along the jaw. Still he didn't lift his hands, although the blow knocked him off-balance.

Mitch came in fast then, pumping hard driving punches at Sherill's chest and face. And now Sherill's hands did come up. But instead of hitting Mitch he crossed his arms in front of his face and Mitch connected there solidly only once.

Sherill was taking punishment lower down and involuntarily lowered his arms to his chest. Then one of Mitch's looping roundhouse swings caught him on the side of the head and he fell sideways to his knees.

Mitch stood waiting, breathing heavily. When Sherill didn't at once come to his feet, Mitch swore feelingly, said, "Fight, damn you!"

Sherill said, "No. But you can have your fun." And, smiling broadly, he came to his feet again.

Mitch swung on him once more and he

turned his head so that Mitch's knuckles only grazed his mouth. Then, quite suddenly, Mitch stepped back and lowered his hands, asking, "What the hell is this?"

"You tell me," Sherill said.

"Why didn't you let me take you on in to Ed like I wanted?" Mitch asked hotly. "Why'd you do what you did?"

"Because of what Ed would think. The way it turned out, he's sure of you. Remember the other night?"

"What about it?"

"Ed wanted you to take care of me. You wouldn't. If we'd gone in there with both of us in one piece today, he'd right now be sure you and me were playin' the same hand."

Grudgingly, Mitch admitted that this made sense. But the thought of his beating still rankled and now he said, "No one ever did that to me. Not that easy."

"That was luck. You left yourself wide open."

There was the hint of a smile in Sherill's eyes and Mitch was thinking, *I still ought to beat his ears back.* He said belligerently, "It couldn't happen again."

"Who said it could? I was lucky."

Mitch was disappointed. He wasn't even getting an argument out of this. To cover his momentary confusion, he asked testily,

"What the hell are you after up here?"

"Just looking out for myself."

"With Ed Stedman as a side-kick?" Mitch asked acidly. "You're sure particular who you travel with."

"The same goes for you."

"Like hell! Ed's crooked, a killer. I may be on a lonesome, but I don't buy into anything like that. This is just a handy place to hide out. When I want to pull out, I'll ride. Ed don't swing any big stick over me. You saw what happened the other night when he tried."

Sherill reached down now and beat the dust from his knees, drawling, "You and I might work something out, Lockwood."

"Such as what?" Mitch's glance was wary.

"Such as finding out who tells Ed what to do."

Puzzlement showed on Mitch's blocky face.

"Somebody does," Sherill went on. "You could keep an eye open and find out. And let me know."

Mitch smiled thinly. "Ed'll like to hear this."

"If you tell him."

Mitch was thinking, *Whatever his play is, he's telling me more than he should.* He was puzzled as he asked, "What else could I do for you? If I would."

"Let me know if Ed leaves the layout. Find out where he goes and how long he's to be gone."

"How do I let you know?"

"Go to Whitewater and hunt up Ned Rawn. Anyone there can tell you where to find him. Give him any word you have for me."

Mitch gave Sherill an uncomfortable look, saying, "You're a damned fool to be tellin' me all this."

"Why?" Sherill lifted his wide shoulders. "A man has to trust someone."

"Why me?"

"Call it a hunch. Call it anything you want."

Mitch didn't like this, didn't like it a bit. Yet from somewhere deep inside him rose a small run of excitement. "Then you're up here after Ed? You're not throwin' in with him?"

"That's about it, Lockwood. I'm here to break him."

"For a reason. What is it?"

Sherill's instinct had all along been to trust this man. Now he saw no reason to doubt his judgment and he said, "Because everything I own is up there in Ed's corral right now. Sixty head of horses. I'm up here after them."

Mitch breathed, "No!" incredulously.

High in the timber along the ridge that

overlooked this basin stood a thickset man, tight-holding the reins of his horse. He had been watching Sherill and Lockwood and presently, for a full five minutes after they had gone their separate ways out of the basin, he stood there thinking about what he had seen, understanding little of it but knowing that it was important.

Caleb Donovan shortly rode on along the ridge, keeping well clear of the trail as he always did when he came in to see Ed Stedman and give him his orders.

IV

Caleb Donovan tied his horse far up the slope and went on afoot, moving awkwardly because of his thickset bulk. When the cabin and bunkhouse came into sight below, he moved from tree to tree and presently had the cabin between him and the bunkhouse, thus somewhat relaxing his need for caution.

He stopped finally behind a tangle of scrub-oak above the cabin and threw a thumb-nail-sized pebble so that it struck the cedar-shake roof and rattled lightly down across it. Shortly, Ed Stedman appeared around the cabin's corner and stared up into the trees. Donovan stepped into sight and Ed immediately started toward him.

Waiting there, Donovan took a fresh tooth-pick from his pocket, idly wondering where he'd thrown the old one away. He couldn't remember, for he had been wholly engrossed these past twenty minutes in thinking of that meeting between Sherill and Lockwood that he had witnessed from the ridge below.

"Might as well come on down," Ed Stedman said as he approached. "No one's around except Slim. And he's asleep."

Donovan shook his head, saying briefly, "Up here," and led the way back up through the trees. He and Ed had argued this before and he had his way, intending that no one but his foreman should ever know that he came here.

Now, behind him, Ed said, "Plenty's happened since you were here last."

"Sherill, you mean?"

"So that's his name, is it?" Ed's tone was surprised.

They climbed a bit farther, until Donovan could no longer see the cabin below. He stopped finally and sat on a rotting windfall, breathing hard as he told Ed, "I know part of it. Sherill was picked up in town yesterday with that mare of ours you borrowed. Why would you let him ride her in that way?"

"Let him!" Ed laughed softly. "Hell, he just did it." And he began telling Donovan about the past two days, about Sherill.

Presently they had pieced together their stories and Donovan was saying, with a touch of admiration in his tone, "He's got brains, Ed. Take that idea of handling horses through Rawn. I know Rawn. He wouldn't think of touching anything off color. Sherill's damned clever."

"We could do worse than to hang in with him, Captain."

Donovan's glance slipped around, bright with sudden anger. "You were never to call me that!" he said tonelessly. "Never!"

Ed's face flushed. "Guess I forgot for a minute," he said quickly and in some confusion.

"You did. Don't do it again." Donovan spoke almost mildly, but there was a plain enough meaning behind his words.

An awkward silence hung between them now and for a moment Donovan was uncertain of this man as he thought back upon that unsavory period in his past, five years ago, when he hadn't known from one day to the next whether the Army was going to bring him before a court-martial or accept his resignation. Finally he had been able to cast enough suspicion upon his Supply Sergeant, who had already deserted, to clear his name officially. But he had left the Army suspected by his fellow officers of accepting bribes, of falsifying accounts and of padding inventories.

He was guilty of all this, as was the sergeant. He had made a four-year attempt to go straight. Last year the offer of managing his niece's ranch had seemed a guarantee to an honest future. But late last year Ed Stedman, his sergeant, had tracked him down. There had never been any mention of blackmail between them. Ed had simply stayed on in Whitewater, not working, just waiting. This hideout had been Donovan's idea, a natural outgrowth of opportunity, of his wish to use Ed in some way, and of his greed.

Now his thought was, *I'll have to get rid of him soon, when this is finished.* Aloud, he said, "We can work this hard all summer. Then we quit."

"What'll Sherill think of that?" Ed asked.

"Does it matter what he thinks? How much of a share did he want?"

"Half of everything beyond wages."

Donovan nodded. "How soon can you leave?"

"Where to?"

"North. To find a layout up there like he wants."

"I could get away tomorrow."

"Good. Leave Purdy in charge. Tell him to play along with Sherill but not to do anything till you're back." Donovan thought of something that made him frown. "I'd feel better about it if I knew what went on between Lockwood and Sherill."

Ed shrugged his flat shoulders. "Mitch had his dander up. You say he took a few swings at Sherill and — "

"But they talked afterward. For maybe five minutes."

"Sure. Sherill had to prove he was in with us."

Donovan's frown eased somewhat, not entirely. "I still don't like it. Have Purdy keep an eye on Lockwood."

He stood up now, a smile crossing his face as he said, "Ed, this time we don't make any mistakes. Not any. We leave all the outside work to Sherill."

"That's the way he wanted it."

Donovan nodded. "Did you see that bunch of horses we brought in three weeks ago?"

"I don't think so."

"He don't get a cut on those, Ed."

They talked a few minutes longer. Then Ed turned and walked back down through the trees and Donovan, watching him, was thinking that if Purdy turned out to be handy at working the crew he might soon be able to forget his worries about Ed and what Ed knew.

By mid-afternoon on that day Jake Henry had crossed the barren and torn low-country that isolated the foothills and was well up in the pines, pushing his mule faster than she usually travelled. By four o'clock, he was high in the hills and occasionally within sight of the south trail leading down from the hideout. An hour later, along a ridge that flanked the trail, he was out of the saddle and carefully studying sign, the tracks of a shod horse with a toed-in right front shoe.

Must be Sherill, he told himself. He had never before seen this particular set of tracks and that meant something, knowing as he did, by sign, most of the animals ridden by Ed's crew. So now he felt no little satisfaction in having proved out his hunch that Sherill had come back up here alone today.

It was as he would have expected. Sherill was keeping wide of the trail and would probably make a circle before coming in on the hideout. Approving of these tactics, Jake followed the sign.

A quarter-mile further on, high in the timber overlooking an open basin, he came to a point where the needle-matted earth was freshly scarred in many places, telling him that the rider he was following had spent considerable time here.

He was about to ride on when he saw the heel-print.

It brought him aground and to his knees, closely studying it. Except for the Army, men in this country who rode horses didn't wear a flat-heeled boot. This mark had been made by an Army boot or one like it. Curious now, musing, *No, it isn't him after all,* Jake looked around more deliberately.

He found Caleb Donovan's quill toothpick on the ground near the thick stem of a pine, along with clear bootprints. He stuck the toothpick in the frayed band of his flat-crowned hat, and when he left the spot he swung wide of the sign, knowing he was close to the meadow and not wanting to come onto this other man, whoever he was.

Presently he was looking down on the two cabins, the barn and the end of the meadow with the big corral at its foot. He stayed there a good half-hour, until the thickening dusk hid what lay below.

At the beginning of that long interval he saw Ed saunter down out of the trees and disappear into the small cabin nearby. Immediately afterward, very remotely, he thought he heard the sound of a horse being ridden away, down-country. He didn't pretend to understand the sound except that it tied in with Ed's unexpected appearance and the presence of that rider he knew had come in along this ridge this afternoon.

Much later, he caught various glimpses of Mitch and Slim, the latter walking with a decided limp. At dusk, four riders came up the trail and were turning their horses into the corral when another pair joined them. All this time Jake was closely watching the bunkhouse. Beyond not seeing Sherill, nothing indicated that he was down there. Neither the small cabin nor the bunkhouse were being guarded.

The clanging of the cook's iron at the cookshack made Jake's mouth water. He waited until everyone — the men at the corral, Ed from his cabin, Mitch and Slim from the bunkhouse — had gone to eat. Then, thinking of his empty stomach and of the jerky and cold biscuits in his saddlebag, he mounted the mule and made a wide circle down to the trail.

As he went on, the shadows deepening about him, he was feeling a mixed disappointment and relief. The disappointment came in not having found Sherill, the relief in being fairly sure that Sherill hadn't stubbed his toe and wasn't being held by the crew back there at the hideout.

There was only one thing to do, Jake decided. Tomorrow, at dawn, he would begin watching the layout again. Sooner or later Sherill would show up.

For the first time today he was struck by the oddity of his trying to help a man he had good reason for hating. Obtusely, instead of hating Sherill, he respected him.

His liking for Sherill was based on his instinct for admiring the finest of a species. He had good evidence that Sherill was exactly that. Yesterday his pride had been deeply hurt when he thought he had misjudged the man, when he saw Sherill with Mitch and Slim. Last night's brawl in the saloon, and their talk afterward, had corrected his false impression. He felt good about the way it had turned out. Wanting to help Sherill through this trouble came as natural to Jake as wanting to pull a fine stallion from a bed of quicksand.

Now, regardless of his hunger, Jake wanted to put plenty of distance between him and the hill-ranch. It was already dark and, after half another hour's steady riding, he swung up through a stand of aspen and away from the trail, the starlight laying tricky shadows against the night's cobalt void. Presently, far back from the trail, he dipped into a ravine and across a narrow creek. He was working up out of the ravine when he smelled smoke.

He stopped, catching a stronger trace of burning cedar riding the slight breeze coming out of the south. The fire lay below him along the gorge. As he came down out of the saddle he was thinking of the rider he had followed along the ridge this afternoon, thinking that this might be that unknown's camp. Jake wanted a look at him.

After tying the mule, Jake worked fast down the slope above the timber-choked depression. He moved with a stealth acquired through many years of stalking game, soundlessly, his moccasined feet stirring up only faint whispers lost in the low murmur of the creek.

He had gone four hundred yards when he caught a flicker of light through the leafy aspens in the ravine's depths. Closer in, he could see the fire's gleam in under a rock overhang that jutted from the steep wall opposite. The fire lay at the lower edge of a circular open break in the trees.

He worked around so as to come in on the fire from below. On his wary circle he passed close to a horse staked out in the grass at the lower edge of the open ground. The horse was watching him. He jumped the creek a hundred yards below the fire. He hadn't yet seen the man.

The overhang was broad, perhaps ten feet above the level of the ravine-bottom. Jake worked as close in to it as he dared, finally lying flat behind a thorny thicket, holding the Navy Colt's in his hand now, thumb on its hammer.

He could see a fry-pan sitting in the coals. An empty tomato-can lay nearby. The odor of cooking meat was strong and made his mouth water.

Suddenly from above a drawling voice sounded down: "Let me know when you get tired of playin' Indian, Jake."

The wolfer's head jerked up and he saw Jim Sherill up there peering down at him, head and shoulders showing over the edge of the overhang.

As Sherill burst out laughing, Jake swore and came erect, feeling ridiculous as he rammed the Colt's back in holster and brushed the dust from his front.

He said testily, "Let me make a damn' fool of myself! Why didn't you sing out?"

"It was too much fun watchin' you, Jake. The sorrel got jumpy five minutes ago. I wanted to see how good you were."

Sherill was still laughing as he slid down from the near end of the overhang and came over to the fire to join the wolfer. "Maybe this meal can make up for it," he said. "Fall to. You look hungry."

They split that first portion of the jerky and tomato stew, Sherill dumping another can of tomatoes and a handful of jerky into the pan for a second go-around. If Sherill saw anything odd in Jake being here, he didn't mention it.

Finally Jake went to the stream and sanded

out the pan and, as they were waiting for the coffee to come to a boil, he asked, "Any luck today?"

"Some. I was in there. I can go back whenever I feel like it."

Jake knew that there was more to this than Sherill was telling. That could come later, he decided.

Just now he had something else on his mind and asked, "Would you know a jasper up there that wears a boot with a flat heel? That would keep shy of the trail and that would leave a thing like this lyin' around?"

He reached up to his wide hat, took the toothpick from the band and tossed it across.

Sherill picked up the quill, looking at it, an expression of seriousness slowly settling across his angular features.

He said, "Lots of men use these things, Jake."

The wolfer shrugged, making no reply.

"But the boots," Sherill drawled. "Flat heels?"

"It was there, plain on the ground."

Sherill drew in a deep sigh, saying, "Today, down below, I met a man that wore a flat-heeled boot. And he was using one of these on his teeth." . . . He looked across at Jake . . . "Major Donovan. Ever hear of him?"

Jake thought a moment. "Don't he run

135

one of those outfits down across the river?"

Sherill nodded. Then his look became uncertain. He tossed the quill into the fire, reaching for the fry-pan, drawling, "Have some coffee! Hell, it couldn't be Donovan. I'm so spooky I'd suspect my own mother right now."

"Of what?" Jake asked.

While they drank their coffee, Sherill told him.

The next day it turned sultry and hot and there was the feel of mid-summer in the lifeless air.

Jean was washing the noon-meal dishes when the Major rode in from the town road to the corral. In a few minutes she heard him enter the office. Although she was curious and anxious to talk to him, she finished the dishes and straightened up the kitchen before going in to see him.

"Jean, you're damned handsome. More and more like your mother," was his way of greeting her.

He came from the window and pulled the swivel-chair from the desk, offering it to her, saying, "I think Jacobs will take our offer. He's writing me. Those steers don't look too bad."

It was unlike him to be this affable and

as she sat down she wondered what lay behind his manner. Fairly sure that he was lying about having seen Jacobs or the culls, she now baited him mischievously and deliberately, asking, "How's the new school coming over there?"

"Slow," was his noncommittal answer.

"Do the Jacobs kids still have that Shetland?"

"Didn't notice," he said. "A few more buys like this and we'll be on our feet again. By the way, Rawn seemed to have a lot of good things to say about Sherill."

"I expected that. Was he the only one you saw about him?"

"The bank. They say he can swing it."

Now, thinking of Sherill, Jean for the moment forgot her doubt of the Major. "Did Sherill mention what he was going to put on that grass?" she asked.

"Horses," Donovan told her, unable to miss the opportunity of smoothing the way for what he knew was coming.

Abruptly she remembered her reason for being here and looked up at her uncle, asking, "Who was the new driver on the stage yesterday afternoon? I'd never seen him before."

"Here either," he replied.

She knew now, definitely, that he hadn't been to Sands. He knew Ben Towers as well as she did. Rising from the chair and going to the door, she held her excitement nicely in check, saying, "Maybe it's a good thing you went over there after all."

"He'll sell to us," he said as she went out.

She wanted to see Brick now, to tell him what she knew. But, knowing how strongly the Major resented her attachment to the old cook, she knew it would be better to wait.

It was sunny and hot outside, and she decided to work in the yard. She went out to the wagon-shed and mixed a batch of whitewash and when Sherill rode in just after two o'clock she was painting the garden fence.

He shut the gate and led the sorrel over, drawling, "You're not afraid of the sun," as he smiled down at her, noticing her bare head.

"It doesn't hurt the plants, so it shouldn't hurt me." She answered his smile. "Would you like to see the Major?"

"No. You'll do."

He dropped the reins then and leaned against the unpainted stretch of the fence nearby. "Just wanted to ask if it was all right for me to move into the shack down on the river. I've got a man down there now lookin' around. Can I leave him there tonight?"

"Of course. It's not very comfortable. No beds. Have you seen it?"

"Just now," he said. "We'll make out all right."

She reached up to brush aside a loose strand of hair and left a smear of whitewash across her brow. Suddenly he was smiling broadly. She felt the moistness on her forehead then and rubbed at it and when he burst out laughing she could no longer suppress her merriment, laughing too.

"You'll have it all over you before you're through," he said. "Want some help?"

"And spoil the fence? No thanks."

"There's only one way of takin' that. I quit," he said. Then, thinking this light-hearted moment as good as any for settling what he had on his mind, he asked casually, "Has the Major been away?"

She looked around quickly, her hand pausing in its stroke and hanging motionless. "Yes, but why should you ask?"

He shrugged. "Just wondered if he'd been to town to draw up that lease. I was headed in there and thought I could sign it today. When was he in — yesterday?"

She nodded and turned back to her work, wondering *Why should he want to know this?*

immediately seeing that only because of her suspicion of the Major had there seemed anything odd about Sherill's question.

But a moment later when Sherill drawled, "That must've been him I saw along the road a while ago," she once more suspected that his curiosity was no ordinary one.

She laid the brush across the top of the pail and faced him. "Just what are you trying to say?" she asked.

"Not a thing," he replied.

He knew then that he couldn't deceive this girl in this clumsy way and he went on, smiling guiltily, "Or maybe I am. You see, I've lost a bunch of horses, a big bunch. They were run off up into the hills and now I've found 'em. There's a thing or two I'm not straight on and — "

"And you think the Major had something to do with it?" she asked. She was angry now, her strong sense of pride and family loyalty crowding her to a defense of Caleb Donovan she knew was wrong the instant she had spoken.

"Miss, I didn't say that. I was only thinking you might — "

"You're thinking exactly what I say you are!"

She knew that she was voicing her own suspicion of the Major, not Sherill's. But fear was strong in her now, a fear that she had at last stumbled upon the explanation for the Major's strange absence.

She wasn't admitting a thing. This was strictly a family matter, nothing for a stranger to have a hand in. So strong was that deep pride in her that she could think of nothing but the need for quieting Sherill's suspicions.

So now, before he could speak, she lied, "The Major was in Whitewater yesterday afternoon. He was back in time for supper. Now if you'll be so good as to take your troubles somewhere else, I'll finish what I've started here."

He gave her a long and searching look that was wholly grave, finally drawling, "I'll ask your pardon, Miss. Maybe I was thinkin' some things I shouldn't."

"But why would you think them?" she asked, as he turned away and sauntered out to swing astride the gelding.

"The reasons wouldn't interest you."

Her curiosity brought her away from the fence and over to him. She had to know what it was he was thinking, what he had found out about the Major.

She looked up at him and tried to put a real warmth in her smile as she said, "Perhaps they do interest me. If you're in trouble, they most certainly do. After all, we're . . .

at least we're neighbors."

"Tell you about it later, when I know more." Sherill's dark eyes bore the trace of a smile as he reined away.

Jean stood there watching as he rode through the gate. Then, quite suddenly, a panic hit her and she turned and ran across the yard to the cookhouse, not caring that the Major might be watching from the office window.

Caleb Donovan didn't see her. He hadn't even known of Sherill's visit. Ever since Jean had left him he had been standing at the room's other window, staring out toward the town road yet seeing nothing as his thoughts played with the possibilities opened up by his talk with Ed yesterday evening in the hills.

Now, as Jean went to the cookhouse, a movement out there along the trail cut in on his ponderings and the vacancy left his stare. A buckboard was coming in along the trail, the driver and a passenger sitting the seat.

Less than a minute later, Donovan had identified the man beside the driver as being George Lovelace. A strong sense of alarm struck through him. He picked up his hat and went out into the yard. He was standing at the gate when the buckboard swung around the corral and headed for the yard.

When the vehicle drew to a stop, Donovan nodded civilly to the driver, a townsman he knew. Then he looked up at Lovelace, saying, "How are you, Commodore?" sensing that no good was to come from this meeting.

"Couldn't be better, Captain," Lovelace said with his usual hearty smile. He climbed awkwardly from the seat, using the wrong foot on the wheel-hub as he swung aground, complaining, "Thank the good Lord I don't often have to travel this country. Riding one of these things would kill a man in less than a week."

He came over to Donovan, they shook hands, and he said, "Just wanted a talk with you, Captain. Won't take a minute. Where can we go?"

Without a word Donovan led the way on up along the fence and back toward the corral. He stopped at a point that was well beyond hearing of the townsman, so placed that he could see the yard and the cabin. Then he asked, "What's on your mind?"

"Business," the Commodore replied, his smile now taking on a sly quality. "Money for you and value for me."

Donovan said nothing but stood there eyeing the smaller man warily, waiting.

Shortly Lovelace went on, "I hear you're

leasing part of your place to a man by the name of Sherill."

Donovan nodded, nothing more.

A shrewd look crossed Lovelace's face. "Captain," he said smoothly, "we know enough about each other so that there's no use beating about the bush. Am I right?"

"That's correct, Commodore."

"Then I'll state my proposition. It's simply this. As you probably know, Sherill has lost some horses. He proposes to get them back again and hold them here on your place until they're sold. If his plans work out," he went on, too absorbed in what he was saying to note the unbelieving look that crossed Donovan's face, "it's worth a thousand dollars to me to see that he loses his horses again before they can be sold."

Donovan stood there too shocked to speak. Lovelace's last words had entirely escaped him, so violent was his surprise at having discovered what Sherill really intended. *They're his, that whole damned bunch up there in the big corral!* was his thought now, anger boiling up in him.

Lovelace misread his look and quickly said, "Come now, Captain. In the old days I greased your palm often enough. It's still not too late for the Army to be interested in what I could tell them."

His words jarred Donovan back to some semblance of sanity, the threat in them stemming the cold fury that was gripping him. "How much are you offering?" he asked flatly. "And what's it for?"

"A thousand was my offer. To see that Sherill loses his horses again if he finds 'em."

The confusion in Caleb Donovan's mind worked against his giving a straight answer now and to gain time he said, "This is blackmail, Lovelace."

"It's no such thing!" the Commodore bridled. "It's a simple business agreement. I have good reason for wanting to break Sherill. That reason's none of your affair. Some years ago I kept my mouth shut when you were in trouble. You owe me something for that."

"Maybe I do," Donovan drawled, in control of himself once more. "When would I get the thousand?"

"Afterwards. After you've driven off Sherill's horses."

"I'll take half now, the rest afterwards," Donovan said.

"No," Lovelace said flatly, sure of his ground.

Slowly Donovan's tight-faced look faded before a smile. He said, "I think you can count on it, Commodore."

Later when he came up to the house after

145

watching the buckboard until it was out of sight, he found Jean waiting for him on the porch.

"Who was that, Major?" she wanted to know.

"A man who owns a river boat," he told her. "He'd heard about our losing all those cattle and wanted to buy hides. I told him it was too late."

Back in his office the Major sat for a long time thinking of Sherill. He winced as he realized how close a thing this had been. But presently he could smile. Lovelace had unwittingly done him a favor. He experienced a small regret at realizing that he would never be collecting the Commodore's thousand, for now that he was forewarned he could deal with Sherill and move the horses deeper into the Breaks.

Tomorrow, he decided, *tomorrow I'll go on up there and tell Purdy what to do.*

Then he began wondering what sort of an excuse he could give Jean for being away tomorrow.

Ned Rawn took more than usual pains with his appearance that night as he got ready for the Lovelace party. He had gone to Kelly's for a bath and a haircut and now he brought the lamp over to the bureau and combed a little pomade into his moustache.

146

Then he meticulously clipped two strays hairs that were out of place over his right ear. He was careful when he pulled on the pressed gray pants. He dusted his highly polished boots. Finally he tied his tie that was two shades darker than the suit.

He was a vain man and after he had pulled on his coat and buttoned it he went to the mirror again, shrugging his bony shoulders so that the coat-collar hit the back of his neck just right. He gave his hair a final smoothing, thinking, *You look it, even if you aren't,* picked up his hat and went along the hallway to the Lovelace's door. Having just reminded himself of how broke he was — he had lost most of that borrowed thousand last night — he was trying not to think about it.

Ruth answered his knock, pulling the door open and stepping back for the effect it would have on him, saying petulantly, "They've left me all alone, Ned. Dad's down there on the boat fussing with things. He even took Lou. She wasn't here to help me dress."

"Then you should always do it alone," he said gallantly.

Her smile was quick and happy. "You like it?" she asked, holding out the flowing white skirt and turning daintily around for his inspection.

He invariably searched out the unexpected thing to say to a woman and now was no exception. "Lucky devil," he drawled.

"Who?" Ruth was plainly startled.

"Jim."

Her face took on a flush of pleasure at his indirect compliment. But then she turned serious long enough to say, "Let's not think of him tonight, Ned. I want so much to be happy for a few hours."

"I'll see that you are, Ruth."

He helped her into her light velveteen wrap, letting his touch linger at her shoulders, and when they went down onto the street she took his arm, laughing gaily at something he said. In front of the warehouse directly below, the street lay in near-darkness and he drew his elbow in tighter, pressing her arm. She came closer to him and he could feel the swell of her breast against his arm and the sudden lift of his desire was a thing he had to fight down.

They rounded the end of the warehouse and before them lay the *Queen* brilliantly lighted by her own lanterns and what others George Lovelace had been able to buy at the two hardware stores. During the day the big sternwheeler had been moved up and away from the littered stretch of the levee and now lay with her bow stage resting on a smooth approach of clean-swept gravel.

Presently they sat down to a dinner far and away the best Ned had ever eaten in Whitewater — fried chicken and country ham, corn pudding, creamy whipped potatoes, squash, rich gravy, pickles and relish, white wine with the main course and after the apple-cobbler, a heavy port, all delicacies that came from the *Queen's* boiler-deck coops and bins that had been stocked in a richer country than this.

It was a gay gathering, ruled by the Commodore's boisterous talk and hearty laughter. All these people were his friends made over ten years of successful trade along the upper Missouri and if one or two felt that they had paid dearly for his services they forgot it as the food and the wine mellowed them. To most of them the gilt-decorated and polished dark panelling of the saloon, its crystal-pendant chandeliers, the deep-upholstered chairs, the maroon carpets and the flowered china were seldom-seen luxuries. So for a few hours these twenty-odd men and women were forgetting the drabness of their lives and enjoying this to the utmost.

Ruth sat at her father's right at the head of the heavy laden oval table. Across from her Ned Rawn divided his attention between looking at her, talking to George Lovelace and dropping an occasional word that kept a constant stream of talk flowing from Judith Ledbetter, the judge's attractive daughter. The judge occupied the chair facing Lovelace at the foot of the table, and by the time the wine made its fourth round his tight face had reddened and lost its reserve and his seldom-heard laugh was gustily challenging the Commodore's.

Time and again Ned caught Ruth's eye and drew a smile from her. She would invariably let her glance drop, avoiding his. Tonight, having made up his mind to something, Ned was keenly aware of her physical attraction and he sensed that she realized it. Once she caught his glance on the white roundness of her bare shoulders and, as he lifted his eyes and looked into hers, he smiled faintly and she didn't look away and some unspoken thought passed between them.

He went around the head of the table when the meal was finished and told her, "Let's go look at the river, Ruth."

She laughed softly, happily, as though they shared some secret. She led him out onto the deck and up the steps to the texas, high above the dark river. She stopped abruptly and before he expected it, and he came roughly against her, his arm automatically reaching out to steady her. She turned into the bend of his arm and her face tilted up to him, suddenly grave.

He saw nothing to make him hesitate and he kissed her. He could feel her breathing quicken and slowly her arms came around him and then there was no reserve in her.

Shortly he drew his head back and looked down at her, saying, "I've known for days that this would happen, Ruth."

"So have I."

He kissed her again, this time in the ungentle way of a man no longer hiding his hunger. Music all at once echoed up from the saloon below. Neither of them heard it.

At about the time Lovelace's guests were finishing the second course of their dinner, Jim Sherill was wading his gelding in to the levee several hundred yards above the *Queen*. The boat's deck-lanterns laid bright fingers of light across the dark water and, observing this, Sherill thought wearily, *Just one more thing*, deciding that this late activity could mean but one thing. Lovelace was loading the boat and would be leaving on the downriver trip in a day or two.

He hardly cared. The thought that he might have seen the last of Ruth did little to deepen his depression and, matter-of-factly, he now accepted this possibility along with the other disheartening one the afternoon had brought him.

He had been a fool to let his curiosity over Donovan take him to Anchor. Donovan right now probably knew every word of his conversation with Jean Ruick. If that were true, he had lost every advantage a month's work had given him. Ed's crew would once more be on the hunt for him if he ever again rode those hills. Which meant that tonight he was even further from his goal than he had been when he last saw the Lovelaces.

The sorrel lunged up the levee-bank and Sherill threaded his way through the maze of merchandise strewn across the broad expanse of ground. Further along he saw the dark shape of another boat, no light showing. He rode the alleyway between two of the warehouses and, coming upon the street, passed a nearly-finished brick building and read the legend on its cornerstone, *First Territorial Bank, 1879.* Then he was in the jam of the night-traffic, the sorrel tossing his head in nervousness at the noise and the movement around him.

Sherill's glance idly roved the crowded street and just as idly he was wondering whether he'd eat or drink, possibly break a long-standing habit and drink a lot. Maybe

Ned could help out there. The prospect of seeing Ned somehow eased his worries.

He left the sorrel at Kramer's lot and afterward turned out onto the crowded walk, losing himself in this town's odd assortment of humans. Here were wide-hatted riders like himself, somber clothed professional men and gamblers, overalled homesteaders and miners and prospectors fresh off the river boats, women dressed more gaily than those who frequented the street by day. The saloons were going full blast, the barkers shouting from their high stands. Sherill could smile thinly as he passed the *Fine and Dandy*, noticing the burlap that hung across the glassless windows.

He was a higher and wider shape than most along this walk and, because of that and the clean look of him, a young woman stepped out of the shadows of a dark alleyway and came in beside him and took his arm, saying, "Haven't seen you before. Just come in?"

"Just." He looked down at her with an open smile and made no move to withdraw his arm. "Some town."

"The worst there is," she said in a hard way. A man roughly jostled her but she took no notice, matching Sherill's slow saunter, adding, "Except for one or two places

I could show you."

"Some other time," he said.

They moved into a store-window's pale wash of light and her thin and painted face tilted up at him as she asked petulantly, "What's wrong with tonight?"

"Something else on."

She sighed, slowly withdrawing her arm from his. "You looked different," she said, not pretending now. "Lately I've had all the bad luck there is."

She turned away and he stopped, watching her fade back into the shadows. "Not quite all," he breathed, wishing too late that he could have told her just that.

There had been a grim note of conviction in her voice that now blunted the thin edge of his self-pity and, as he went along the walk, he could think back more rationally upon those minutes with Jean Ruick that had so changed things for him.

He was exactly where he had started three weeks ago. Thinking of George Lovelace's ultimatum, he almost laughed. He wondered what the Commodore would say now if he knew how things stood. And, wondering, he decided that he would tell him. Tonight. Now.

He was taking a perverse satisfaction in imagining what their meeting would be like as he climbed the steps to the wide veranda of the *River House*. Then he was remembering how Ruth had come down here to give him that parting word as he left two nights ago, remembering it and thinking how odd it was that he hadn't once thought of it since. Today, as yesterday, Jean Ruick had been in his thoughts more than any other person and it suddenly came to him that ever since meeting her he had unconsciously been making comparisons between her and Ruth. Now it made him uneasy and a little angry to realize that, because he had so seldom thought of her, Ruth must have suffered by these comparisons.

He thrust all these disquieting uncertainties aside as he went along the upper hallway and knocked on Lovelace's door. There was no answer.

His disappointment was short-lived before the prospect of seeing Ned, and as he went back along the corridor he could even feel a small relief at not having to face the Commodore just now.

Ned's room was dark, empty. He struck a match and had a brief glimpse of the room's disorder, the bed unmade and a rumpled suit lying on it. He caught the sweetish odor of the pomade and idly thought, *Who's the lucky girl?*

He asked for Ned downstairs at the desk. "Try that boat down on the river," the clerk told him. "Lovelace is giving some sort of a shindig tonight."

Now he knew the reason for all the lights on the *Queen* and as he came back onto the street and turned down past the warehouse toward the levee he had given up the thought of seeing Ned and was instead wondering if he could find Ruth, get her away from her father and have a real talk with her.

He walked quickly up the wide stage and onto the feebly-lit boiler deck. Two crewmen, Negroes, were lying on a mound of baled hides and watched him incuriously as he picked his way through the tiers of close-packed boxes and barrels and climbed the broad companionway to the hurricane deck. There were lights up there, and as he rounded the fore-end of the cabins he found several people standing at the rail looking off across the river, the colorful gowns of the women at odds with the Sunday-best suits of the men.

He spotted Tom, Lovelace's colored boy, coming toward him carrying a tray of glasses. He waited there, asking as the boy came up, "Tom, where'll I find Miss Ruth?"

"Up above, suh," the boy told him, giving his toothy grin.

Sherill thanked him and walked down past the group at the rail and turned up the narrow steps climbing to the texas.

Once his head was above the level of that top deck the lights from below were blocked out and he was staring into a darkness only faintly relieved by the glow coming from the head of the street. He hesitated there, looking on past the cabins and along the low-railinged deck.

Then he saw them standing there in the deep shadow of the texas, Ruth's white gown blending into the darker outline of Ned Rawn's gray suit. Their backs were to him and he could see Ned's arm circling Ruth's waist.

All at once a constriction was in his throat and his head had a swollen, near-to-bursting feeling of uncontrollable fury. He stood there several seconds, wanting to be sure, feeling a knife-edge of disbelief and bitterness cut into him. His face was paling and bleakly set as he finally turned away and went back down the steps.

He was turning into the wide foredeck stairway when he met Tom again. The boy looked at him and asked, "You feelin' bad, Mist' Sherill?"

"Nothing I won't get over, Tom," Sherill answered, going down the steps.

This galling bitterness was something he had never before experienced, brought on solely by having witnessed Ned's betrayal of him. Oddly enough, he could feel little surprise over Ruth. The pattern of her shallowness and insincerity stood out in dozens of small things now etched with startling clearness against this background of deceit. All that remained of his feelings for her was a self-loathing at his own blindness and shallow wants.

But Ned stood for something different, for something far more deeply-rooted in his past. He was remembering all the fun they'd had, all their fiddle-footed wanderings and all the hard work that had bound them in sure and easy friendship. Yet he had just seen something that made all these things meaningless. To realize that this Ned wasn't the one he had known in the old days was no salve to his feelings.

He walked up between the warehouses, glad for the quiet and the darkness here that were letting him get a new grip on his thinking. Dispassionately, without a trace of self-pity, he looked at all the facts.

He had come to Whitewater to marry a fine girl, to meet an old friend, last of all to make a little money. Today he had lost his chances at the money and he cared so little about it that now he could shrug that knowledge aside. He had lost Ruth and in so doing had discovered himself lacking in discrimination, a disquieting fact he must always guard against. But what stuck deepest, jarring the foundation of his belief in his judgment, was Ned's turning against him. He couldn't understand it, couldn't begin to see the reasons behind it.

He was coming up along the walk fronting the hotel veranda when a man sitting at the far corner of the railing saw him and came erect, calling in a low voice, "Sherill?"

When Sherill stopped, Mitch Lockwood climbed over the railing and swung down to the walk, saying, "I played a hunch and hung around. Rawn wasn't in."

"No," Sherill said, staring down curiously at the shorter man, asking, "How did you know my name?"

"Ed," Mitch said, his look surprised. "Why?"

"Nothing. What's on your mind?"

"Ed's gone north. Left around noon. So I came straight on down to let you know."

"Fine." Sherill tried to sound grateful even though his thought was, *Why bother about that now?*

But then a cold and wicked anger was in him at so mildly accepting this long run of

159

bad luck. Tonight he had had proof of certain flaws in his judgment where Ned and Ruth were concerned. Just now, perhaps, he was too hastily misjudging another situation. He was giving up too easily. Stubbornly, angrily, he told himself, "The hell I will!" saying it aloud.

"The hell you will what?" Mitch wanted to know.

Sherill laughed, unaccountably relishing a thought. "Nothing, Mitch. Nothing." Then, more soberly, he drawled, "We're going up there after those horses, Mitch. Tonight."

V

Sherill and Mitch rode those forty-odd climbing miles to the hill-ranch in a little more than five hours. Sherill had thought of going on to the river line-shack to get Jake but had given up the idea as a waste of too much time. He had set a killing pace all the way up through the timber, Mitch at times falling far behind. Then finally the sorrel had given out and Mitch had caught up again and they were together when they came to the foot of the meadow. It was long after midnight and the ghostly light of a waning moon laid tricky shadows through the pines as they approached the cabins.

On this long ride, the core of Sherill's resentment had burnt itself out to be replaced by a near-forgotten urge of wild recklessness that harked back to the old carefree days with Ned. But tonight that reckless urge was tempered by a cooler judgment and a definite hardness that was something he had never before experienced.

"Wake 'em up," he told Mitch as they drew near the bunkhouse. "We move out

161

right away. When you're ready, call me. I'll be up in Ed's place."

Mitch asked, "How do you think you're goin' to swing this? Purdy's a cold-blooded devil."

"I'll take care of Purdy. Tell him I want to see him."

Sherill went on toward the small cabin, Mitch to the bunkhouse. Sherill heard someone call out and, as he swung aground, saw a lantern's glow in the bunkhouse window.

He went into Ed's office and lit the new lamp in the bracket above the desk. He went on into the other room a moment, giving it a cursory glance that showed him nothing but a bed, two chairs and a wash-stand made from a packing-crate. Back in the office, he set the lamp on the desk and opened the drawers, going through them quickly.

He was looking for something, anything, to tell him more about Ed and the man who bossed Ed. His thoughts about Donovan were neutral now, waiting to be swayed either way. He admitted that he was reserving judgment of the man only because of Jean Ruick, because of his strong instinct for liking her and his unwillingness to believe badly of anyone so close to her.

He was pulling out the desk's big bottom drawer when a furtive step at the door brought his glance up. A slat-bodied rider of middle age stood there, a man whose light hazel eyes were beady with controlled anger and suspicion as he drawled:

"Mitch says you wanted to see me."

"You're Purdy?" The man gave a grudging nod, whereupon Sherill asked tersely, "Where did Ed put the bills of sale on those horses?"

"There never was a bill of sale on the place."

Purdy had a face that was immobile as a slab of granite. Only his eyes betrayed his wariness of Sherill. He wore his gun as Sherill did, low along the right thigh. One thing definitely hinted that he had come here cocked for trouble. The fingers of his right hand were spread open more than those of his left, not quite relaxed.

Sherill saw all this, then heard the scuffle of boots in the yard beyond Purdy. He knew at once that the others were watching this, that he would have to make his play for the horses here and now, that Purdy was the man to make it against.

So he kicked shut the bottom drawer of the desk, impatiently drawling, "How in hell do I make a trade on these horses without a bill of sale?"

"Ed said to sit tight. We don't move any horses till he's back."

Sherill came around the end of the desk now, almost within reach of the man. "If we wait that long we lose the chance."

"Then we lose it."

Sherill asked, "Didn't Ed tell you about me?"

"Yeah. But he didn't mention anything bein' on the fire."

"What if he didn't? Does that mean I can't make a deal? Go on, get your men ready and we'll move out."

Purdy's stare narrowed a little as he drawled, "The hell with that! Those horses stay — "

He saw what was coming and his hand clawed up along his thigh, really fast. Sherill hit him with a full swing, wanting to hurt him. Purdy's Colt's lanced halfway into line but suddenly dropped as his head snapped back to thud hard against the door-frame. His frame buckled and he sprawled loosely out across the door-sill.

Sherill stepped over and toed Purdy's inert bulk out so that he rolled off the step and onto the ground.

"Mitch," Sherill called, "You're in charge. Get that corral open." Then he deliberately turned his back on the door, going around behind the desk once more.

He heard an angry voice mutter something

out there and for a moment nothing would have surprised him. Then Mitch's voice drawled, "You heard what he said. Let's move."

They drifted away, their steps fading in the night's stillness, and Sherill stopped holding his breath.

Sherill stayed in the office a few minutes longer, going through that last desk-drawer and discovering nothing that told him any more about Ed than he already knew. Finally he went over and lifted down the three carbines from the wall-rack, then blew out the lamp. He picked up Purdy's Colt's on the way out and walked over into the trees and dumped all the weapons into a thicket.

He mounted the sorrel and rode out past the barn and up to the big corral in the meadow. Vague shapes moved against the blackness and he found the crew working the horses through the gate.

He reined in alongside a man he couldn't recognize in the faint light, curtly telling him, "Cut me out a fresh one."

"Sure thing," came the willing answer.

Once a rider wheeled in out of the blackness and in the brief glimpse he had of the man Sherill recognized Slim.

A quarter-hour later he was riding a big-chested bay, one of his own horses, helping push the herd from the gate on south out of the foot of the meadow into the timber.

Long after all sounds of the herd's going had died out, Purdy staggered over to the bunkhouse, rolled a few things in a blanket and went to the small corral for a horse. Presently he headed up along the meadow, riding at a stiff jog and fighting down his nausea, his aching head letting him wonder how long it would take him to catch up with Ed.

Early the next morning Brick and Jean left Anchor's barnlot in a buckboard, Brick holding the team of grays in to a stiff trot. It was cold, with a wind out of the north and the sky heavily overcast. They took the turning off the trail into the road and then the wind wasn't in their faces and Jean sat a little straighter, no longer hunching her shoulders against the chill that seemed to congeal her thoughts, suspending the need for making the decision she knew she must make before reaching town.

Presently Brick's dry voice sounded over the singing rattle of the buckboard's iron tires. "He ain't acting any different, youngster. Quit worryin'."

It was Brick's habit to break long silences in this fashion, remarking on a thing without preliminary, leaving it to his listener to puzzle out what he was talking about. Now, Jean knew he referred to the possibility of the Major having seen her yesterday when Sherill left, when she had run over to the cookhouse.

So she said lifelessly, "It doesn't really matter."

"Maybe not. But he'd have been in askin' me about it if he was wise to what's goin' on."

"What is going on, Brick?"

He reached over and slapped the mare across the rump with rein-ends before he said in seeming irrelevance, "This Sherill now. I'll lay my bets with him."

"You've never even talked with him. How can you know what kind of a man he is?" Asking the question, Jean wondered why, when her instinct was to believe in Sherill, she had to take this opposite attitude toward him.

"I got eyes, ain't I?" Brick asked. "When you've seen as many men as I have, you get to know the right ones."

"But how could he say a thing like that about the Major?"

"You said it, he didn't. The way you told it, you jumped down his throat before he had a chance to say anything."

She nodded, knowing she had done exactly

what Brick was saying. But that same fear she'd felt yesterday was in her now and she said, low-voiced, "Whatever the Major's been doing, it can't be that he's a common horse-thief, Brick."

"Why did he leave the Army? A man just don't up and quit a job like that at his age."

"He might have had a perfectly good reason."

"He don't drink. And if he gambles he's pretty quiet about it," Brick went on musingly, paying no attention to her remark. "So it was something else that kept him away those times. And where'd he spend night before last?"

"I wish I knew," she said wearily.

He looked around at her. "Get over this idea that none o' your flesh and blood can do anything wrong."

"I'm over it, Brick. If there's a range detective in town, I'm going to tell him what I know."

"Tell Sherill what you know."

"No, I'd rather do it this other way."

Brick retired behind a gloomy silence and they went on following the bend the road took toward the river. They left the rolling grassland and dipped down across the flat of the river bottom and it was where the road turned west again that Brick pulled the team down to a walk, looking off toward the north, toward the river.

"Something movin' off there," he said.

In a moment Jean saw what he meant, saw the haze of dust perhaps a mile distant that obscured the green fringe of cotton-wood and willow marking the river's line.

"Horses," Brick told her.

"Could it be Sherill?" Jean caught Brick's shrug and on sudden impulse said, "Let's go over and see."

Brick at once lifted the reins, turning the team off the road.

In another minute they could see the horses plainly. There were quite a lot of animals strung out and heading east toward the range Sherill had leased. Soon they were close enough to distinguish a man working the near flank of the herd. Then a tall rider on a bay appeared out of the dust of the drag and came toward them.

It was Sherill. Sight of him laid a quick embarrassment through Jean and she said hastily, "Let's go on, Brick."

He gave her a thinly amused glance before deliberately pulling the team in to a stop, drawling, "Let's see you eat your crow like a lady, youngster."

She knew how stubborn he could be and

she had to sit there watching Sherill ride in on them.

Then she halfway forgot her embarrassment as she saw the change in Sherill. A two-day growth of beard shadowed the square lines of his face. As he rode in on Brick's side she saw that tiredness lined his face with a gravity that was reflected in his eyes, and she wondered what had brought the change in him.

He lifted hand to hat as he drawled, "You're out early."

She nodded. Then, knowing Brick was waiting for her to speak, she said humbly, "I'd like to apologize for yesterday. It wasn't very nice of me."

A brief smile touched Sherill's eyes. "Those things happen. I should've kept my lip buttoned."

"Then you meant what I thought you did?" she asked, that fear of yesterday at once striking through her again.

"Suppose we forget it." He tilted his head in the direction of the herd. "There are the horses. So it's wound up all right."

His answer was anything but satisfactory and Jean was about to tell him so when Brick asked, "Have much trouble?"

"Not much. But we're short-handed."

"There's three men sittin' around our place

170

with damn' little to do," Brick went on with a surprising garrulity, and Jean sensed that he was purposely talking to keep her from speaking. "They're yours for the askin'."

"We'll make out." Sherill looked at Jean. "That money of yours will be in the bank today."

Once again, before Jean could speak, Brick inserted his word. "There's some extra beds stuck away in the tool shed. Better help yourself."

"Brick, will you let me say something!" Jean put in angrily. Then she told Sherill, "I'm glad it's turned out so well for you. But I must know something. Did the Major really have anything to do with your losing those horses?"

"Jean, that's a fool question to — "

"Did he?" Jean asked insistently, cutting in on the old cook.

Sherill regarded her without his expression breaking from its seriousness. He was thinking, *She's proud and it would hurt her.* So he said, "I tried to tell you yesterday you'd taken off on the wrong foot."

"There," Brick said triumphantly.

"Yesterday you started to say something about the Major," Jean said, ignoring Brick. "What was it?"

Sherill shook his head. "If I did, I forget

171

now what it was."

Brick gave Sherill a look and a nod of approval.

So, when the girl said, "Try and think, can't you?" Sherill touched the bay with the spur on the side away from her and the horse took several quick steps out from the buckboard.

He pretended to discipline the animal, jerking the reins so that the bay tossed his head and nervously sidled even further from the rig. "We'll talk it over later," he called and, lifting his hand, let the bay go.

As he cantered obliquely over toward the herd, he was wondering who Brick might be and how much the old man knew. He obviously did know something. What that something was Sherill intended finding out. He would ride across to Anchor the first chance he got and have a talk with him.

Just now he and Mitch were having their hands full with the horses and, coming up on them, he could see that they were straggling. During the night the impact of his authority had worn off and, one by one, Ed's crew had slipped away in the darkness. He had halfway expected that some such thing might happen and it hadn't mattered much, since the main need he'd had of them was only in getting clear of the hideout. But it was tedious work now for only two of them to handle these sixty head of horses and when he finally came up with Mitch, who was see-sawing across the drag trying to keep the animals moving, Mitch said relievedly:

"Five more minutes and they'd have been spread clear across the country."

"An hour more ought to do it, Mitch." Sherill pulled his neckpiece up over his face and got to work.

The bay knew this business, not waiting for a touch of the spur to turn back some animal trying to leave the bunch. So Sherill put his thoughts to other things. He was feeling better about Jean Ruick now that he'd seen her again. He couldn't explain the incongruity of his not having asked her if she had told the Major of their conversation yesterday. Back there he'd thought about it and, on the point of asking, had checked himself with the queer notion that to ask would offend her. He had been strongly inclined to believe just then that she had somehow treated the matter as a confidence between them.

Now he wasn't so sure. After all, it didn't matter with the horses safely out of the hills. So, he put from his mind the thought of their misunderstanding and remembered the

173

way she had looked, her face reddened by the chill wind and brightly alive and altogether beautiful. For the first time he admitted that she strongly attracted him, that he was hoping something would smooth out the troubled course of their acquaintance.

During last night's long drive out of the hills he had often thought of her, wondering which of half a dozen excuses he could use for riding over to Anchor this morning. Now he regretted that their meeting was over, that he couldn't be sure of finding her at Anchor if he did ride in there later.

So finally he dismissed that idea, deciding to help Mitch work the horses as far as the line-shack where Jake had been waiting since yesterday afternoon, then to leave Mitch and Jake with the herd and go on in to Whitewater. He would sign the lease, make his payment on it and then go find Ned.

He hadn't let himself think too much of Ned and Ruth this morning. But now he was suddenly impatient to see how Ned would act when they met. He had tried time and again to think of some logical explanation for what his friend had done, had failed to find one. Yet a slender hope that there was that explanation, and that he could discover it, was what was taking him to Whitewater.

He wanted to believe in Ned as much as

he had ever wanted to believe in anything.

The gusty wind ran off the peaks under the leaden clouds and hit the river-bottom with a cold spasmodic violence. By midday it was whipping the dust along Whitewater's main street, scattering bits of paper and rubbish, worrying the animals along the hitch-rails and the people on the walks. Today had the makings of one of late spring's freak-ish storms and the freighters that crossed the choppy river on the ferry and headed out the Arrow Creek road were wondering how long it would be before their heavy wagons were up to the axles in mud.

Down along the levee, the small stern-wheeler that had arrived yesterday was disgorging her cargo. Above, thirty-odd men were feverishly loading the *Queen*. George Lovelace would occasionally appear on the hurricane deck to shout something down to his mate, taking in all this activity with an impatient eye.

Just past twelve Jean Ruick came down the outside stairway from the *Cattlemen's Association* offices over the bank. She walked along to where Brick waited by the buckboard in front of the courthouse and he helped her up onto the seat and they drove straight out of town.

Had Jean come along the walk five minutes later, she would have met Ned Rawn hurrying along carrying a new alligator-hide suitcase. Ned was stopped three different times by men along the walk and all three passed a cheerier word than usual with him and shook his hand in parting.

At the *River House,* Ned went up to his room after taking a lot of good-natured joshing from a group of men in the lobby. An hour later, he had his back to the door when someone knocked. He didn't even turn as he called impatiently, "Come in."

Jim Sherill stepped in the door and was closing it before Ned faced around to see who it was.

Sherill was watching him closely and first saw his face redden deeply, then saw him drop the stack of shirts he'd been holding in one hand.

Too affably, Ned said, "Where you been keeping yourself, stranger? Thought I was going to miss you. Sit down. Here, let me make room."

He lifted the suitcase from the room's one chair, moving the chair out from the bed onto which he had emptied the contents of the dresser, a small brass-bound trunk and a battered war-bag.

"Goin' somewhere?" Sherill asked as he

took the chair. He sat in it backward, long legs thrust out and arms folded over its back.

Ned had recovered from his momentary confusion and his smile was genial as ever now as he said, "Am I! All the way down the river."

Sherill was surprised. "That'll take time. When do you get back, next fall?"

"Never, if I have any luck. Jim, Lovelace has offered me a job. I'm going with the *Queen*."

Sherill sat straighter. The news of the *Queen's* departure he had halfway expected. But Ned's going was a real surprise. "Thought you had a job," he said.

"I have." Ned turned serious. "But there's something you don't know about, Jim. Nothin' to do with the job. You see . . . Well, hell, you might as well know. I've been hittin' the cards too much. This crowd won't let me alone. Now I'm stone broke and figure it's a good time to quit. If this other works out, I'll never have to look at another card."

Sherill was on the point of reminding his friend that the Mississippi country was also card country. Instead, he merely said, "Maybe I'll see you down there."

"Man, if you only would." Ned's tone lacked the heartiness he intended. "We could tear Hannibal apart. How soon do you figure to make it?"

Sherill shrugged. "Soon now. We brought the horses down last night."

Ned's eyes opened wide. "Jim, that's the best news I've had in a long time," he said, his enthusiasm strangely unconvincing. He thought of something, quickly asking, "Have you told Ruth and the Commodore?"

"Not yet."

Ned seemed relieved. "You haven't much time. The *Queen* leaves in the morning."

"Then you've got some work to do." Sherill rose, thinking *If they wanted me along, he'd be saying so now*. He said, "This leaves me high and dry for ninety days. Until I can deliver the horses."

"Who cares how long it takes you?" Ned asked, again with that forced geniality. "By the way, this morning I mailed a letter to Dave Ramsay at Fort Selby. Told him you were the best man with horses I'd ever known. All you have to do to get in the remount business is go over there and see him and get the keys to my desk from Kramer."

"But now that I've got the horses back that's all changed, isn't it?"

"Maybe it is," Ned said, adding, "Of course, if anything should happen, you could

178

always take up where I left off."

"Just what could happen, Ned?"

"Who knows? You might even decide not to come down to Hannibal for another year."

"Is there any reason you know of why I wouldn't?" Sherill was watching his friend closely now.

"Not a one." Ned forced a smile, saying with a false gusto, "And you'd better not trump up a reason."

Sherill took out his tobacco, rolled up a smoke and tossed the sack to Ned. As they lit their cigarettes from Ned's match, Sherill drawled, "Wonder where I can find Ruth?"

Ned shook his head. "No tellin'. Maybe she's down on the boat by now. I've heard a lot of moving around up at the other end of the hall."

"Go ahead with your packin'," Sherill said.

As Ned turned away, Sherill stood looking out the window across the back lots, his thinking almost idling as his conviction strengthened that Ned was deceiving him in something beyond the thing he already knew. There had been no mention of the party last night. And Ned's enthusiasm for his coming on to Hannibal was obviously forced. Something was wrong here, 'way wrong. Ned was acting like a boy caught stealing a fresh-baked pie from his mother's kitchen. Slowly, surely, that depression and fury of last night was settling through Sherill again.

Finally he could no longer stand the turn his thoughts were taking and he sauntered across to the door, saying, "See you later. Maybe I'll go say goodbye to Ruth and the old man."

"Hope you can find them," Ned said.

Sherill stepped out into the hall asking, "You're sure about this, Ned? Sure you want to go back there and never see a hill higher than your hat? That country's all fenced in."

Ned sighed and threw out his hands. "Who said I wanted it? Lovelace has thrown a good job my way. If it doesn't work out, I can always come back. Besides, you'll wind up there. If it's good enough for you, it'll suit me."

Sherill smiled briefly. "Okay. You always did have a mind of your own."

He turned toward the head of the stairs and Ned called after him, "So long," and he lifted a hand, not turning, noting that Ned hadn't offered to shake hands.

The bar downstairs was crowded and Sherill went in there and bought a drink, thinking he might see Lovelace. But he hadn't by the time the drink was finished and he went out onto the street half-decided to go down to the *Queen*. In the end he changed his mind, not knowing exactly why, and turned up-street instead, nursing his anger and bewilderment, restlessly wondering how much basis there was for his distrust of Ned beyond what he had seen last night.

He was passing a hardware store when someone called his name and he turned to see Fred Spence coming down off the doorway step. The sheriff came over to him saying, "Thought you were going to keep in touch with me, Sherill."

Jim Sherill was in no mood to make excuses, so he simply said, "That's right, I was."

Spence gave him a look more of amusement than anger. "Never mind, Ned explained things," he said with an abrupt warming smile. "Did you have any luck with the horses?"

"Some."

"If you need me, all you have to do is holler," Spence said quite cordially. Then he thought of something: "By the way, what do you think of Ned marrying the Lovelace girl?"

It was as though he had thrown a hard blow at Sherill, although there was nothing visible to show it. Sherill stood there so long without speaking that Spence gave him an odd look. And Sherill's words were quite toneless as he said, "Hadn't heard about it."

The sheriff said heartily, "Well then, get

181

on down there to the hotel and hit Ned for a cigar. They were hitched this mornin' at the church. You should've been the first to know."

Sherill nodded. "I should, shouldn't I?" he said, and turned away.

Fred Spence couldn't understand it. Instead of going toward the hotel, Sherill headed in the opposite direction. The sheriff would have been more puzzled had he seen Sherill riding out of town some minutes later.

Purdy had travelled slowly during the night and at dawn, with the high-country blanketed in cloud, he was tempted to turn back. But he was nursing a deep hatred of Sherill that outweighed the prospect of any physical discomfort and when it started snowing he pulled on his slicker and kept doggedly on.

He had been through here twice before with horses and followed the only way he knew, keeping generally north and remembering his landmarks well, even though the country was shut in and he could catch only infrequent glimpses of the higher peaks. He was as hard on himself as he was on the horse, stopping only once in the next two hours to build a fire and spend a few minutes thawing himself out.

If he hadn't reasoned that Ed would be

laying over in this foul weather he might finally have turned back. But his hunch that Ed's camp was closer than the hideout was strong enough so that, toward the middle of the morning, he was only faintly surprised to see the orange glow of a fire ahead through the fog of lightly falling snow.

He rode straight on in, came out of the saddle and without ceremony went up to the blaze to warm himself. The fire lay on ground kept dry by the spreading branches of a lofty balsam. Purdy was sure that this was Ed's camp and that Ed had either seen him coming or heard him and was now probably playing it safe. And, shortly, Ed Stedman came walking in through the trees.

Ed took one look at him and asked, "What the hell hit you?" Purdy told him.

Ed listened without once interrupting. When Purdy had finished, Ed was deep in thought and walked over and broke up several branches to toss on the fire before saying, "You should've had more sense than to buck him. This may be the best hand we've held yet."

Purdy gave him an angry look. "Damned if I see it."

"Suppose Sherill really had a buyer for those horses? You say he was lookin' for bills of sale."

"Pawin' through your desk. I nearly let him have it! Now I wish I had."

"No," Ed said patiently, "you should have stuck with him, played along until you were sure of one thing or the other. If it was a real sale, then you wouldn't of made a fool of yourself. If it was a steal, you'd be there now to swing the thing our way."

Purdy only glared at him, making no answer. Finally Ed shrugged and said, "So now we go back. Ten to one you've wasted two good days of my time. And Sherill won't like that." He unrolled his slicker, pulled it on and trudged out after his horses.

They broke camp half an hour later, Ed leading his pack-horse and not liking the prospect of this long ride.

At about the time Sherill left Whitewater after seeing the sheriff, Jake was riding the foot of the draw where he and Mitch were holding the horses. The herd had settled down and there was little to do beyond turning back an occasional animal drifting toward the river.

Jake and Sherill had picked this spot yesterday, a quarter-mile wide sweep of good grass separating two low ridges between which a willow-rimmed creek snaked its last mile to the river. In his cautious way Jake

184

had so far kept clear of Mitch, following his natural instincts even though he was impatient to learn how Sherill had managed the seemingly impossible in bringing his herd out of the hills. Finally now, after these four hours, his curiosity had become so strong that he headed the mule out across the draw to where Mitch sat his horse below the ridge to the east.

Coming in alongside Mitch, he asked, "You on your way back up there tonight?"

"Not tonight or ever," Mitch said.

"So it's that way, is it?" Jake didn't try to hide his astonishment. He realized that there was a point beyond which his curiosity couldn't go openly. So he drawled acidly, "I would be down here last night instead of up there."

"It was a pretty thing to see," Mitch admitted.

"It would be if Sherill had anything to do with it. There ain't a better man alive."

"I'm beginnin' to believe that."

There was one way to find out about last night, Jake saw now, only one. So he told Mitch, "Time was when I thought I could twist the tail of anything from a mountain cat to a real mean longhorn. Then I tangled with Jim Sherill and learned different. He persuaded me to leave Yellowstone country as soon as I could walk afterwards."

Mitch looked puzzled. "You two had a run-in?"

"We did. A real one. Maybe I could lick him with a knife. But I wouldn't even be too sure of that. Anyway, this time I speak of we tossed all our hardware away and just went to work on each other."

Jake tilted his head over, lifting a hand to point to a white scar along the line of his jaw. "Sherill did that. With his fist. Must've hit me there twenty times. Just picked that spot and kept after it. Finally it jarred my knees loose. It was three days before the knees were worth a damn."

"What brought all this on?" Mitch was grinning now.

Jake shrugged. "I'd been eatin' deer meat so long I'd worked up a sharp taste for beef. But I picked the wrong critter. It was Sherill's. He caught me dressin' it out. He couldn't see it my way, so we got into that disagreement."

Mitch was softly laughing. "Maybe I know how you felt."

"And maybe you don't," Jake said ruefully.

"If I don't, then Purdy does."

"Who's Purdy?"

"The *segundo* up there. Last night he couldn't see it Sherill's way about movin' these nags out. So Sherill rocked him to sleep."

"Where was Ed Stedman all this time?"

Mitch eyed the wolfer queerly. "You know Ed?"

"By sight. I run my traps up in the hills."

"Then you've seen me?"

"Sure. A man has a right to pick the place where he draws wages. Now you've picked this one. A good move."

"Sherill's not payin' me wages," Mitch bridled. "I wouldn't take anything for this."

"Me either," Jake said solemnly.

Mitch took that in, then said, "Ed left the layout yesterday. I let Sherill know and he made his play. It worked."

Just now his glance went beyond the wolfer. Something caught his attention and his stare narrowed as he asked, "Who's that?"

Jake looked back over his shoulder to see a thickset rider crossing the foot of the draw along the river four or five hundred yards below.

He had his careful look at the man and finally said, "That would be Donovan. He runs this outfit."

Mitch at once lost interest. "Now all Sherill's got to do is hang onto this herd for another ninety days and his worries are over."

"So he told me," Jake agreed idly. His attention was still on Donovan, who was now disappearing beyond the foot of the opposite ridge. He was thinking back on what Sherill had said about Donovan night before last at their camp in the ravine. Sherill hadn't been at all sure of that hunch about the Major.

Now, on sudden impulse, Jake told Mitch, "Think I'll take a look around. Can you get along without me for a while?"

"Sure. These jugheads won't stray," Mitch said.

It was Jake's way to be furtive about a thing like this. So he told Mitch nothing of his intentions and rode out the head of the draw instead of taking the much shorter way along the river. Once out of Mitch's sight, he kicked the mule to a faster trot and began a wide circle that finally brought him back to the river a good mile above the foot of the draw. He started down toward it with the mule at a slow walk, as though riding aimlessly.

Donovan wasn't in sight and Jake made two long casts over toward the river-bank without picking up any tracks, which meant that Donovan hadn't come this far. That in itself struck the wolfer as being queer, as indicating that Donovan wasn't on his way up the river as it had seemed when he and Mitch sighted the man.

He was abreast a half-acre grove of cotton-woods when he abruptly came on fresh sign and knew it to be Donovan's. The sign lined out straight for the trees, which grew clear to the river's edge. Jake noted that but drifted on past the cotton-woods, still holding the mule to that indolent walk. Anyone watching him would have thought that he was riding quite aimlessly.

He continued on and, crossing the foot of the draw, looked up and saw Mitch where he had left him and waved. He went on beyond the lower ridge and around a gradual bend of the river. When he had gone far enough so that he could see nothing but the opposite bank of the bend upstream, he kicked the mule to a run and headed for the river, not caring that it was so deep here that the mule would have to swim. He was in a hurry.

He took a wetting to his waist before reaching the far bank, all the while thinking back on what he knew of this section of the bad-lands he was heading into. Once across the river, he swung the mule sharply downstream. He covered a quarter-mile at a hard run, still well out of sight of anyone who might be watching above the bend.

Finally he struck a high-walled wash and turned away from the river, still running the mule. This wash lifted sharply and at its head opened out onto a wide wind swept flat. He held the mule to a fast trot all the way across the flat and then, in the hills beyond it, swung sharply west, up-river.

Forty minutes later, after a series of swings that took him much deeper into the hills, he stopped the badly-blown mule and walked up to the crest of a low rise. Just short of the crest he went to hands and knees and crawled the last five yards. He picked out a low-growing cedar, crawled in behind it and looked over into a shallow coulee.

Along the bottom of the coulee ran the definite line of a trail, lighter in shade than the surrounding ground. Jake spent a good five minutes studying the trail above, where it lifted out of the coulee. He was finally satisfied that no dark markings showed on the trail. To him this meant that no one had travelled it for the past several days.

He crawled back down the slope and again took to the saddle, this time riding leisurely only a quarter-mile. He stopped the mule again in a stunted clump of yellow-pine, from this point looking down and out across a stretch of ground he knew the trail crossed.

Ten minutes later he saw Caleb Donovan

top the lip of a wash a good quarter-mile below. And for the three minutes Donovan was in sight he considered which of several choices to take, once muttering aloud, "Now why the hell didn't I let Lockwood in on it?"

His discovery had him excited. Here, to Jake, was proof of what Sherill suspected. Donovan was on his way to the hill-ranch, which meant that he must be the man who had gone up to see Ed Stedman two afternoons ago. It was important that Sherill should know about this. But wasn't it even more important that Sherill should know why Donovan was riding up here today? The Major had obviously seen the horses. What was he going to do about having lost them?

Jake carefully considered the time involved. It would take him at least two hours to get in to Whitewater. Supposing he missed Sherill? Even if he found him, it was a good six-hour ride back up to Ed Stedman's layout. And in that length of time Donovan might already have started his move, if he was to make one.

He had to go on, Jake decided, get up there and watch the layout and see what happened. Only when he knew what was to happen should he see Sherill. No sooner was the decision made than he was astride the mule again and heading up-country.

Not once in the next three hours was he within sight of the trail Donovan travelled. He made good time, knowing these hills. He was on the ridge above the layout when Donovan rode in a little after four o'clock.

It was cold and gray and the wind whipped down across the meadow rippling the tall grass so that it looked like a choppy lake. Jake shivered against the still-damp chill of the buckskin. But what was going on below soon made him forget how uncomfortable he was.

Within two minutes of Donovan's arrival, several men had appeared from the bunkhouse and from the corrals. Ed Stedman and Purdy were the only ones Jake knew by name, although three of the others were familiar to him. Ed and Donovan were the center of the group that stood by the bunkhouse door out of the wind.

It didn't take long, whatever they decided. In fact, the group broke up before Jake had read their intentions, three men going to the small corral to saddle horses, Ed and Donovan crossing to the small cabin to reappear almost at once, carrying carbines.

Jake got out of there then, climbing higher along the ridge and several minutes later taking a last look down at the layout. By that time all of the men were mounted and heading for the trail. Donovan and Ed were in the lead, their horses at a fast trot.

They're in one hell of a hurry, Jake told himself. Then he suddenly realized what this meant to him. All the men down there were riding fresh horses, even Donovan. And he, Jake, was riding an animal that had already seen a lot of hard work today. All at once he was afraid. The fear came when he saw that they might travel the distance to the river faster than he could.

He dropped to the far side of the ridge and pushed on recklessly and fast, trying to think of ways of saving time, deciding finally that the trail was the quickest and easiest way out of here. So he covered the next two miles as fast as the mule would go. Then he dropped down into the trail. He knew that they would probably see his sign. But it occurred to him that this might work to his advantage, that it might slow them if they discovered someone besides Donovan had used the trail today.

Over the next hour and a half he punished the mule without mercy, much as he hated to do it. Several times he reined in at high points along the trail and looked back. While it was still light, he didn't once sight the men who were following him and with the dusk his hopes lifted a little.

It was long after dark when he finally reached the river and waded the mule across to the cotton-wood clump above the draw. He pushed on down-river, a fast jog the best he could get out of the mule.

He turned into the foot of the draw and bawled, "Lockwood!" reining his animal to a stop, listening for an answer.

No voice answered him over the gusty whine of the wind. He was worried as he realized there was probably not time enough to ride to the head of the draw and find Lockwood.

So he rode across until he came upon a small bunch of horses and started them up the draw. He came to a single animal, pushed him on ahead of him.

He had made three of those back-and-forth swings across the draw, gathering horses and working them deeper between the ridges, when a sound toward the river stopped him.

He sat listening, wondering what it was he had heard. Then warily, he drew his Navy Colt's and swung aground.

Hardly had his moccasins touched the grass when a gun's muffled blast rode down from the head of the draw. The echoes of a second and a third shot were whipped away by the gusty wind. Then he heard the slow-rising mutter of hoof-falls and knew that the horses were running toward him, away from the shots.

He wheeled and peered off into the darkness in the direction of that first sound. All at once a high shape, indistinct as yet, drifted in toward him. A moment later he saw that it was a rider.

He called out sharply, "This is Jake!" lifting his gun.

He saw the rider wheel quickly away. He lined the Colt's and fired, immediately running for his mule. Astride, he swung the mule out after the rider. The animal had taken only half a dozen strides when she suddenly shied violently aside.

Jake reined in, seeing a vague shape lying on the grass. He got down and walked over to it, gun held ready. A man lay there. Bending close, Jake saw nothing familiar in the blurred makeup of the features.

Several horses pounded past as he was going to the saddle again. From up the draw came a rising thunder of hooves now and in his rage Jake lifted the Colt's and emptied it into the air, hoping to turn the herd back. Then the guns above spoke once more and he knew there was nothing he could do.

He ran the mule across to the foot of the east ridge, reloading the Colt's. He was rocking shut the loading-gate when he briefly glimpsed a rider trotting past. He raked the mule's flanks and brought the rider into sight again, having his quick look at the man's shape and knowing it was neither Sherill nor Lockwood.

He lined the Colt's and threw three swift shots, gaining on the rider. He was close behind when the man's shape swayed and toppled from the saddle, the horse wheeling off out of sight. Jake reined in then, listening to the horses running past, a cold and baffled fury holding him helpless.

Out beyond him someone shouted, "Chris! That you?"

Jake headed toward the voice, gun held ready. Over all the racket of the wind and the running horses he finally answered, "Over here," hoping to toll this man in to him.

Hardly had his voice died out when a gun blasted at him sharply to his left. He swung that way, firing at the wink of gun-flame. Then he heard a horse pounding away and knew that he had missed and couldn't follow.

It was over quickly as it had started, the sounds of the running animals dying out toward the river. Jake tried to run the wornout mule down there. But now the animal was completely played out, hardly moving under gouge of Jake's sore heels.

Then Jake heard the remote rolling echo of shots striking in out of the east. The line-shack was off there and at once he was afraid of what he would find as he headed the mule for the ridge.

Jim Sherill rode off the windy west ridge into the draw as the day's gray shadows were thinning with the early dusk. He had forgotten the passage of time before the somber run of his thoughts and now he realized that it had been several hours since he had left Whitewater. He couldn't remember travelling the road or even turning off to come across here to see Mitch and Jake.

He saw Mitch cross the creek and ride toward him and in the minute before Mitch came up to him he tried to collect his thoughts, to shut from his mind the bleak ponderings that had been with him since seeing Fred Spence.

"How'd it go?" he asked as Mitch joined him.

"Easy," was Mitch's reply. "These nags like it here."

"Where's Jake?"

"Been gone since noon. Said he was havin' a look around." Mitch had noticed the lifeless quality in Sherill's voice and was wondering at it as he added, "He must've decided there wasn't enough to keep us both busy. And there wasn't."

"Let's eat," Sherill said then, and reined away.

"Do we just leave 'em?"

"Why not?"

Mitch was willing, for he was hungry and had several times this afternoon dozed in the saddle. So now he fell in alongside Sherill and they started up along the east ridge.

What if something does happen? Sherill asked himself. Briefly, he debated sending Mitch on alone to the line-shack and staying here himself to watch the herd. But then he remembered that the crew hadn't tried to help Purdy last night and that Ed Stedman was away. Without a leader the crew would stay put. Furthermore, he had run a good bluff last night and they might still think that he was one of them. Finally, Jake Henry wouldn't be off somewhere prowling around on his own if he thought the herd wasn't safe.

Once more the things he had learned in Whitewater today took possession of his thoughts and he and Mitch rode the half-mile to the line-shack in silence.

They turned their horses into the small corral with barely enough light left to find the grain-bucket in the lean-to. They were wordless as Mitch got a fire going in the small shack's hogsback stove. Sherill opened another can of tomatoes and added it to the stew in the dutch-oven that Jake had cooked last night, telling Mitch:

"Tomorrow we eat better. I'll pack some grub out from town."

"We could always butcher one of those Anchor steers," Mitch said, grinning.

His hunch that something was wrong strengthened when Sherill let this remark pass. In the light of the candle he saw the tight set of Sherill's face and knew that something beyond tiredness was wrong with the man. He made one more attempt to stir Sherill from his moody silence before they ate. But his levity made no impression and he couldn't even be sure that Sherill heard him.

Finished with the meal, Mitch said, "I'd better get back out there."

"I'm taking the first turn," Sherill told him. "You get some sleep."

Mitch was about to protest when Sherill went on. "This is going to be a long haul, Mitch. It'll be another ninety days before I can sell. Stay with me a week and I'll be set to do it on my own. Before you leave, the best gelding in the bunch is yours."

"Hunh-uh," Mitch said at once. "I got

all I ever wanted out of this last night. Watchin' you make suckers out of that pack o' curly wolves. And if it's all the same to you I'll stick the whole ninety days."

Sherill gave him an odd look. "Then what?"

Mitch lifted his heavy shoulders in a spare shrug. "I'll think about that when it comes along, *amigo*."

Sherill briefly considered that use of the Spanish word. There was something he wanted to know about Mitch and he said finally, "I run a few cattle down on the Yellowstone. The layout's forty miles from anywhere. Would that be too far south for you to hang your hat as long as you want to stay?"

"No. Sounds just about the right distance from Arizona," Mitch drawled with surprising candour.

Sherill nodded, now knowing all he wanted to about Mitch. "I boarded up the place when I left and ran my beef in with a neighbor's," he said. "So there may be some work gettin' started again. There'll be only the two of us to begin with."

"When you left the place you weren't countin' on comin' back?" Mitch asked.

By the sober way Sherill shook his head, Mitch was warned to pursue this line no further.

"Fair enough," he said. "Work's never hurt me yet."

That was the end of their talk and shortly Mitch finished his smoke and spread his blanket in one corner and turned in. It wasn't long before Sherill blew out the candle and went outside. For the few minutes before he dropped off to sleep, Mitch listened to Sherill restlessly pacing back and forth beyond the door, knowing that something was worrying the big man. Mitch's last waking thought was a wish that he could help Sherill with whatever had gone wrong.

No one could have helped Sherill just then. His thoughts had been a monotonous merry-go-round ever since leaving the sheriff in Whitewater this afternoon. He would look back upon his visit to the Lovelaces a year ago and all too clearly remember how desirable Ruth had been during that carefree week in Hannibal. He would look a year further into the past, to the late summer when he had first met Ruth in Cheyenne at the home of her uncle, a cattle-buyer. At first sight of her there had been the conviction that she was the one girl he wanted.

Then there were his memories of the old days with Ned. He would never again smell the scorched hide and the dust of a roundup, bear the bawling of cattle or the quick hoof-drum of a running horse, or look out from some mountain pass across half a hundred miles of country without being reminded in some small way of Ned.

He stood there now, leaning against the corner of the cabin, bareheaded and facing the chill bite of the wind, lost in the bare beginnings of an understanding of how all this had happened. He could see the weakness and insincerity in Ruth now where before he had been blind to her shortcomings. He would be able to forget her, he knew, although his pride was deeply hurt. But Ned was something different. He had long been aware of Ned's quirks and had understood them with never a thought that they could harm him directly.

He was, he decided, too tolerant of the faults in people he really cared for. Yet against his wrong judgment of Ruth and Ned he could weigh his right instincts toward others who had proved out. *Mitch, for instance,* was his involuntary thought, *and Jean Ruick.* Little as he knew Mitch, he was sure of his judgment in having trusted the man. Jean, of whom he knew even less, he couldn't picture as ever being deceitful or inconstant. Beneath her quick responsiveness and changing moods lay a bedrock of intelligence, of strong character. It showed in her face, he had seen it even in the sure and graceful way she carried herself. Now that he thought of it, Ruth was vacillating and her beauty was shallow because there was little depth to her. She rarely put her thoughts to anything except fashionable nonsense. George Lovelace was perhaps the best gauge in understanding Ruth, and he squirmed at the possibilities there, wondering at never having seen certain obvious likenesses between father and daughter.

Quite suddenly now some of the tension eased from his nerves and the rancour in him subsided to the point where he was once again aware of his bone-deep tiredness. He yawned, stretched his long frame and stepped back out of the wind, for the first time today really wanting to sleep and feeling irritated that he couldn't.

He was reaching for the shack's flimsy door when the sharp *crack* of a rifle rode down the wind.

At the same instant a splinter flew from the face of the door close to his hand and from inside the shack came the hollow banging of the stovepipe falling to the floor. Hard on the heels of that sound came the brittle explosion of a second shot. And over in the corral a horse snorted and began wildly pounding around the enclosure.

Sherill lunged through the door, called, "Mitch!" and ran for the corner where he had thrown his blankets. He snatched up his shell-belt from his blanket and was swinging it around his waist as Mitch ran out the door carrying his carbine.

A deafening clang smote the restless silence and suddenly the stove toppled over, the lids rolling off and a shower of hot coals cascading across the floor. Sherill gathered all the blankets and ran for the door as the floor burst into flames.

Off in the west, in the direction of the draw, guns were sounding now. Another shot came from riverward, closer this time. Over in the corral Mitch was deliberately cursing.

Sherill ran to the corral and found Mitch standing by his horse. The horse was down, motionless, and from the far side of the enclosure came the shrill neighing of Sherill's bay and the hollow thudding of his hooves striking the poles.

Mitch cursed again, said, "He got 'em both."

A moment later he lifted the carbine and fired. By the flickering light from the flames leaping before the shack's window Sherill saw a vague shape at the far side of the corral melt groundward. He drew his Colt's and walked over there and found the bay shot through chest and head.

Now the rifle beyond the corral sent its deliberate explosions ripping in out of the darkness. Sherill caught the whisper of one bullet passing close to him and ran back to Mitch, pulling him down so that they lay behind the lowest grounded pole of the enclosure.

The shots broke off, began again a few seconds later from a different quarter. The shack's window jangled apart suddenly and they could hear other bullets ripping through the thin pine slabbing of the walls. The fire was spreading to the roof and shortly they were lying in a strong light, feeling exposed and helpless.

Then, from far off in the direction of the draw, the muted echoes of more shots faintly reached them and Mitch swore time and again, saying finally, "There's last night's work shot to hell!"

The wind was making a huge torch of the shack, the light spreading further outward beyond the corral. Sherill lay looking in the direction from which the shots had come. The rifle out there was silent now.

He saw something move against the curtain of blackness off there and said quietly, "Let's have the Winchester, Mitch," reaching back for it.

He laid the weapon against his cheek and looked along the sights, plain in this light, at the indistinct shape out there. He slowly squeezed the trigger.

The rifle's sharp explosion was muted by the wind and the roar of the flames. He saw the shadow out there move and then move faster.

Abruptly he could hear the quick drumming of hooves.

A horse and a hunched over rider raced in on the corral. He brought the carbine around. But now a bend in the corral's bottom pole suddenly blocked his view and he hugged the ground, saying sharply, "Watch it!"

He had one brief glimpse of that pony, now riderless, running past fifty yards out from the corral. And alongside him Mitch drawled, "Bullseye!"

Much later, after the fire had burned out and they could risk it, they walked out there and found Ed Stedman, dead.

VI

After the dishes were out of the way that night, Jean carried the lamp on in to the living room, lit the second one on the center table and still found the room quite cheerless. The wind was making her restless and now she went out to the porch-corner and carried in some rounds of pine and laid a fire on the wide hearth. When the blaze had caught, the room seemed a little brighter.

Still, she was dissatisfied and stood for several moments looking around with a critical eye, wondering if in white-calsomining the mud-chinking between the logs she could relieve the room's somberness. Except for the square rosewood piano slanted across one front corner, and the small table and slender chair her mother had brought from England as a girl, this was a man's room with many strong reminders of her father. A pair of deer antlers hung on the broad stone chimney above the fireplace and crossed below it were her father's carbine and the sword he had worn at Antietam. For the most part the furniture was heavy and durable, the chairs rawhide-backed. The bright Indian blankets and the red-checked calico curtains were the only splashes of color.

I'll never change it, she decided finally out of loyalty to her father. Her mind made up, she went to her room to get her new maroon-plaid dress. Back again, she sat on the couch facing the fire and started to baste in the hem of the dress.

The wind laid its howling echoes around the eaves to heighten her nervousness and she wondered about asking the Major to close the shutters on the north window.

She had laid her sewing aside, about to go to his room, when she remembered that he hadn't been around this afternoon when she and Brick returned from town. She had told Brick that she wanted to see him when he came in. Brick wouldn't forget a thing like that, which meant that Donovan was still away somewhere.

So she went back to work at the dress, only mildly curious as to what was keeping Caleb Donovan out so long after dark. She tried not to think of him now, for her mind was exhausted from the day-long effort at reasoning out some explanation for his strange absences and for Sherill's strong hint about him yesterday.

She had been discreet in what she had

said to Angus Palmer at the *Cattlemen's Association* office this morning. Yes, he could put a range detective to work for her immediately, any day she named. But what did she want investigated? She had balked there, afraid that her suspicions were too groundless to talk over with a comparative stranger. So she had told Palmer that she would probably be calling on him again shortly.

Then on the way home Brick had talked her into seeing Sherill and having a talk with him before she decided anything about Donovan.

She was thinking back on all this when distant gunshots sounded muffled and faint over the whine of the wind. She sat listening, at first thinking she was mistaken. Then the sound came again, stronger as the wind momentarily died.

She hurried out into the kitchen and opened its north-facing door and she was standing there, hearing a lift in the tempo of the firing, when someone ran past this end of the house and out toward the barn-lot.

Hurrying back to the living room, she threw a coat about her shoulders and was crossing to the front door when Brick's broken step sounded on the porch and the door opened.

"Something's goin' on down toward the river," he announced without preliminary. "Phil and Joe just left to see what they could find out. Now stay here and don't fret about it."

He was closing the door when she said, "Brick." Then, when he opened it again: "Could Sherill be in trouble?"

"Can't tell," he answered impatiently. "Let you know the first thing I hear." And he went out.

She stood listening, hearing nothing now but the whining of the wind. She sat down once more and picked up her needlework. Minutes later, when she found her stitches running two inches out of line, she laid the dress aside and went out into the kitchen and poured herself a cup of coffee.

In that moment was born her first awareness of her real feelings toward Jim Sherill. Suddenly she realized that she was quite miserable and afraid, that her imagining of what could have happened to Sherill was the one thing responsible for that emotion. The intensity of her feelings shocked her at first, then filled her with a glowing warmth until, admitting that she cared deeply for Sherill, she was proud and unashamed.

This was a new experience for her, this intense interest in a man so differed from her last-remembered girlhood romance. She tried to shut out the fear of what might now be happening and to think of Sherill as she had seen him today and yesterday. For several minutes she quieted her restlessness and worry in that way.

The slamming of a door at the far end of the house jarred her thoughts rudely back to the moment and she realized that the Major had just come in. She put the cup down and started into the living room, thinking he might know the meaning of those shots.

Halfway across the living room, a sound coming from the office wing stopped her. She stood listening and heard it again. Someone was whistling. She told herself, *It's someone else,* for never since Caleb Donovan had come to live here had she heard him whistle a note or give anything but his spare smile as an indication of lightheartedness.

Yet the next moment she heard his door open and recognized his heavy tread coming along the short hallway. He was still whistling, softly, tunelessly.

He came on into the room, saw her and stopped. His heavy face was patterned with a broad, unnatural smile and he swayed a little as he stood there.

Then he was saying, quite courteously,

"Good evening, Jean. Brick said you wanted to see me." He spoke in a deliberate way, more slowly than usual and slurring his words.

She said, "Yes. Sit down, won't you?" and watched his unsteadiness as he came over and took a chair. She knew then that he had been drinking.

She laid her dress across the back of the couch and sat down. She was about to speak when a step, Brick's, sounded on the porch and the door opened and the old cook came in.

Brick Chase gave the Major a long look, then glanced at Jean. "Need me?" he bluntly asked.

Jean was watching Caleb Donovan. "I don't think so, Brick."

"Why not?" Donovan asked, still smiling. "Have a chair, Brick."

He pulled back his coat and ran a hand across his vest, having to make two tries for the pocket before thrusting his thumb in it and taking out one of his quill toothpicks. His eyes were heavy-lidded and he seemed to keep them open with difficulty as he tilted his head back and stared at Jean, saying, "Why not have Brick sit in on this? You two've been whispering around together for days now. So why don't both of you put me on the carpet?"

"Major, we'd better wait until tomorrow to talk about this," Jean said, more amused than angry at his insolence. She had never known that Caleb Donovan was a drinking man. She could even catch the odor of whiskey in the room now.

"Wait? Why wait?" Donovan wanted to know. "You've got something on your mind. Get it off."

"You've been drinkin', Major," Brick put in.

Donovan's glance swiveled around and his smile slowly faded. "Who wouldn't, with you two always watching me? Sure, I've been in to town and I've had a few." He looked back at Jean. "You'd like me to quit, wouldn't you?"

"Let's don't talk about it now," Jean said quietly. But at last she was angry.

"Come on. Out with it, whatever it is," Donovan insisted.

Jean gave him a cool regard for a long moment, then said, "All right, I do have something to ask you. Where did you go the day you told me you were going to Sands?"

The Major seemed all at once more wide awake. "Who said I didn't go to Sands?"

"Ben. I went out for the mail that day

and Ben asked about you. If he'd seen you on the Sands road that afternoon he would have mentioned it."

"So?" The Major's face hardened perceptibly. "I have to account to you for my time, do I?" He had worked the toothpick to the corner of his mouth and was talking around it.

"No, you know you don't," Jean said angrily. "But when you pretend to be off looking after my business and then do something else I have a right to an explanation."

"Anything else you'd like to know?"

"Yes," she said hotly. "Why did you lie last winter about being in Whitewater during the blizzard?"

Donovan's glance turned wary for an instant before he caught himself. "Who says I wasn't in Whitewater?"

"Brick went to town the afternoon you got back. He didn't see your tracks in the snow."

"Can't a man ride from here to Whitewater without following the road?" Donovan coolly asked.

"No. The road's the shortest way. Besides, you'd run into fences nearer town."

The Major rose from the chair. He was quite sober and he was sneering openly now as he first looked at Brick, then at Jean.

"So you're taking the word of a couple of broken down old saddle tramps instead of mine, are you, Jean?"

"I'm not. I'm only asking for an explanation."

He stood looking down at her in such an intent way that she was almost afraid of him. Then she angrily thrust aside that small fear and felt nothing but contempt for him. And suddenly the wind's note rose to a gusty shriek and big drops of rain were beating at the window along the back of the room.

Donovan said with a show of dignity, "I'll pack my things and be out of here. Tonight."

Jean was caught unawares. Before she thought she said, "I don't want that. I simply want you to tell me I'm wrong in the things I've been thinking."

"And just what have you been thinking?"

"Many things. None of them things I want to think."

"I won't bother asking you to name them," he said quietly. "I'm leaving."

He turned and she called, "Major, you can't — " She broke off abruptly, seeing that he was ignoring her.

They heard him go along the hallway and then his door slammed.

Brick said, "He looked guilty as hell."

"No, Brick. I hurt him terribly. I shouldn't

have done it. What would mother think of me?"

"I don't know," Brick Chase said quietly. "But John Ruick would be mighty proud of you, youngster."

She didn't look up as Brick left the room and softly closed the door.

Brick was halfway across the yard, headed for the bunkhouse, when he heard the hoof-echo of a running horse sounding across the wind, coming from the east. He turned and hobbled on around the house and down through the cotton-woods, ignoring the needlelike rain that wet him to the skin before he reached the corral.

He was raging inside, hating Donovan, wishing Jean had been more severe, wishing he had two good legs so that he could take care of himself as he had in the old days before a horse had crippled him.

He was waiting there at the corral when a rider pounded in out of the darkness, heading for the cabin. He yelled, "Phil!" and Phil Rust slid his pony to a stop and reined over to him.

"That you, Brick?" Rust was breathing heavily as he spoke down to the old cook. He didn't wait for an answer but went on hurriedly, "Lord, they've got damn' near every steer we own! The wind had drifted most of 'em down into that cut below the new tank and all they had to do was head 'em for the river. Me and — "

"But the shots sounded north," Brick cut in.

"They was. Sherill got it, too. They cleaned him out. Me and Joe saw a blaze off there by the river, so we went that way first. The shack's gone. We found Sherill and one of his side-kicks and two dead ponies. Sherill got the jasper that shot up the shack, killed him."

"Who was he?"

"Never saw him before. But Sherill lost his horses, every damn' one! We'd no sooner got down and was lookin' over the fire than we heard this racket over east. So Joe stayed with the others and I rode across there in time to find 'em drivin' the last of our critters into the river. They threw some lead at me and I got the hell out. A man can't do a thing on a night like this. It's blacker'n the inside of a boot, Brick."

"I know," Brick said tiredly, turning back toward the cabin. Water was running down his face and he said with no life in his voice, "Let's go on up and tell Jean."

"You think I could've done anything?" Rust asked, walking his horse alongside Brick.

" 'Course not," Brick told him. Then he

saw the lantern swinging in behind the trees, the light coming toward them. He remembered Donovan and quietly told Rust, "You go on and break the news, Phil. I'm seein' the Major."

"Is this him?"

"Yeah. Better stay clear of him. He's on the prod."

Rust grunted something unintelligible, but nevertheless eloquent of his poor opinion of Donovan, and reined off into the darkness. Brick stood there watching the swaying lantern, wet and miserable, shivering against the cold, seeing the pattern of what had happened tonight a little more clearly. Donovan had been away most of the day and this fact Brick now placed alongside Sherill's strong hint of yesterday about the man.

Caleb Donovan, wearing a ground-length slicker, almost bumped into Brick before he saw him and took a startled step to one side. Donovan lifted the lantern, scowled at Brick and then without a word went on past him and on in the shed near the corral gate. Brick followed.

The Major lugged his saddle from the shed, hung the lantern from a nail on the gate-post and went in for his horse. Brick came up to the gate and leaned against it, waiting, a cold and killing hatred gathering in him.

Presently Donovan led his saddled bay horse out through the gate. He was closing it when Brick drawled, "You're not so drunk now, Major. Or had I better make it 'Captain'?"

Donovan swung suddenly around and Brick thought he was ready to hit him. Then, typically, Donovan decided to ignore him and turned away.

Brick watched the man climb to his saddle, waited until he had settled himself and wrapped the slicker around his knees. Then: "You didn't mention the fire, Captain."

In the lantern's pale light, Donovan's glance came down and he asked, "What fire?"

"The line-shack down by the river burnin'," Brick said. "If you came out from town, you were within a quarter-mile of it, Captain."

Donovan had looped the reins around his left arm and now thrust both hands inside the slicker as he looked down at Brick, his glance steady and a trifle amused.

He said, "You know I saw that fire, Brick."

"Sure I do." Brick was thrown a little off-guard by this bland admission but said stubbornly, "If you didn't start the blaze yourself, you know the man that did."

"Right again," Donovan drawled. "Ed Stedman picked that chore for himself."

"He picked the wrong one," Brick said

over his strong surprise. "He's dead." Then rage rode in over his surprise, and he added, "So will you be soon, Captain."

Donovan smiled. There seemed to be a little sadness in his glance and in his tone as he said, "Not before you are, Brick."

A hollow explosion pounded the slicker out from his right thigh and the smoke that curled out of the hole in the slicker hung there a moment before the wind whipped it away.

With a brief glance down at Brick, Donovan lifted the reins and rode off into the darkness.

Brick bowed his head, leaning there against the gate-post below the lantern. All at once his bad leg buckled on him and he turned against the post, one arm wrapped around it and his other hand pressing his chest. He let himself slowly down to his knees, moving his head from side to side as though not understanding something.

He lay down very quietly in the hoof-churned mud and didn't move. The only odd thing about the look of him was that his face was buried in a pool of water.

Joe Foote hadn't said much so far tonight. But now, with Anchor's distant lights winking at them through the blur of rain that slanted at their backs, he suddenly started talking to Sherill:

"Maybe this is a bad luck outfit. All them whitefaces pilin' up against that wire last winter. Now all that was left gone. Not enough to do around the place and Donovan chewin' your head off every chance he gets. I'd quit if it wasn't for the girl."

"She's a good reason for staying," Sherill said.

He had been only half listening, his mind on other things, and as the Anchor man's drawl continued over the rush of the wind he no longer even pretended to listen. Instead, he was feeling the faltering gait of Jake Henry's tired mule under him, wondering what luck he'd have borrowing horses for Mitch and Jake and himself from Jean Ruick. He wanted to think of these things, these immediate problems, not trusting himself to let his thoughts dwell on the news Jake had brought them as they waited near the ruin of the shack. The horses were gone, every last animal.

"Hear that?"

Joe's sharp question suddenly caught Sherill's attention and he asked, "What?"

"A shot," the Anchor man answered.

"Missed it," Sherill said, knowing Joe was spooky, liable to hear anything after all that had happened tonight.

Just then, faintly but unmistakably, Sherill caught the rhythmic pound of a running horse going away off to their left and Joe said, "See! By God, let's go!" and he raked his pony's flanks with spurs, sending him on toward the lights of Anchor at a dead run.

The mule lunged to a run as Sherill used the spur. Joe disappeared ahead in the direction of the house as the mule fell back to a trot again. Then against the rain slashing in at his face, Sherill saw the bobbing, moving pinpoint of a lantern's light close below and far to the left through the trees that separated Anchor's yard from the barn-lot.

He angled down there and hauled the mule down out of her job a few yards short of the corral gate, swinging aground before she had stopped, seeing Jean Ruick and Phil Rust kneeling there in the mud alongside a stretched-out figure.

Jean was bareheaded and without a coat or a wrap. He caught her quiet sobbing as he stood beside her and he unbuckled his slicker and took it off and spread it across her head and shoulders. Only then did she seem aware of him, looking around as he knelt alongside, then quickly burying her face in her hands and trying to choke back her crying.

He looked down at Brick and then across at Phil Rust. Joe Foote rode across from the cabin sharply asking, "Who is it?" as he reined in by them. No one answered him and Phil Rust came over to Jean and touched her on the shoulder, saying quietly, "Better come over to the house and get warm, Jean."

She stood up but didn't move away, looking down at Brick a long moment. Then her eyes came around to Sherill. She was still crying as she said bitterly, in a choking voice, "It was the Major. Why didn't I listen to you? Why didn't you make me listen?"

"Now I wish I had," he said gently.

She raised a hand and ran it across her forehead, breathing lifelessly, "I'm sorry. I had no right to say that."

"Better come along," Phil Rust said quietly, and with a last look at Brick she turned and walked away beside her crewman.

Sherill watched them until the lantern Rust was carrying was out of sight beyond the trees. Then he turned and looked down into Brick Chase's face, the lantern on the gate-post above his head hissing softly as raindrops beat against its chimney. He could see that someone had wiped the mud from the old man's face and smoothed his hair back. His expression was altogether peaceful.

Sherill thought irrationally, *You could be*

luckier than any of us, old timer, and was at once impatient with himself. He heard Joe Foote come aground and stand behind him and he knelt down and lifted Brick in his arms, holding him like a child, telling Joe, "Better bring the lantern. I don't know my way around." He started off toward the trees.

They were passing the front of the cabin, heads down against the rain and walking toward the bunkhouse, when the porch door opened and Jean Ruick came out, calling, "Bring him in here, please."

Sherill climbed the steps and she held the door open for him. She nodded to the couch and he crossed the living room and laid Brick down gently, straightening his legs and putting his arms at his sides.

He took off his hat then, stepping over to the fireplace and shaking the water from its wide brim, and Jean said, "There's coffee in the kitchen. You'd both better have some."

Joe, waiting uncomfortably by the door, crossed the room and went into the kitchen and they could hear him say something to Phil Rust in a hushed voice.

Jean had combed out her hair and gathered it at the nape of her neck so that it hung down her back and, though her dark blue dress was spotted and clinging wetly to her shoulders, she was quite beautiful to Sherill.

There was something he had to say before he left her and now he told her flatly, "You might as well hear my end of this. In case you're not sure. Donovan went up into the hills day before yesterday afternoon. I wasn't certain of it then, so I couldn't say anything. But today one of my partners followed him up there again and couldn't get back in time to warn us he was coming after the horses."

"He must have come straight here afterward," she said wearily. "He pretended he was drunk and had been to town." She looked at him gravely, adding, "Thank you for telling me, Sherill."

"People who know me call me Jim," he said. He left her now, going into the kitchen and closing the door.

Phil Rust lifted the graniteware coffee-pot off the stove and filled another cup, handing it to Sherill, saying quietly, "Now she's on her own. Brick was the best friend she had. Her only real one. She shouldn't be in there alone with him."

"She should," Sherill said. Rust took the remark with a quick look at Joe and then an understanding nod.

"Has she any kin-folks?" Sherill asked.

"Nowhere except back East."

"Any friends in town?"

225

"She knows Judy Ledbetter pretty well," Joe said.

"Then somebody ought to take her in there. Tonight," Sherill told them.

He heard the door open behind him and turned as Jean came into the room. They moved aside and she went to the stove, lifting the lid of the coffee-pot and looking into it, asking, "Enough?"

They told her yes and she looked up at Sherill. "So you've lost your horses again, Jim." There was a slight hesitation before her use of his name.

"Again." He smiled bleakly. "And no one to blame but myself. I made a wrong guess."

"Even the horses you were riding were lost, weren't they? Phil told me."

Sherill nodded and she matter-of-factly said, "You'll have to use ours."

"That'd be a help," he told her. "But I'd want to buy 'em, not borrow."

She gave him a puzzled look. "Why?"

"In case you don't get them back."

He caught a trace of fear in her golden-brown eyes as she softly said, "So you're going up there again."

It was a statement, not a question. He didn't say anything.

Her face lost its gravity and there was the shadow of a warm smile for him before she turned away to Phil Rust, telling him, "That big red horse of the Major's would be one, Phil. The paint and the brown are stayers." She looked back at Sherill. "This isn't a sale, Jim. After all, I'm in this now as well as you. And you'll take Phil and Joe with you."

He considered that, at length drawling, "I'll take either one, but not both. One of them is taking you in to town tonight. You — "

"We're taking Brick too, then," she interrupted.

He nodded. "You'll wait in town until you hear from us. Don't come back out here."

Her eyes widened a little in alarm. "You think the Major would come back here? That he'd dare . . ."

She left her thought unworded and Sherill said tonelessly, "All I know is what I saw down there tonight. There and here."

"I'll go," she said at once. "Phil, you'll be with Jim. Take anything you need."

Joe Foote was disappointed and she saw that and smiled, telling him, "You'll have all the luck next time, Joe."

He grinned in embarrassment, saying, "Was I complainin'?"

Phil Rust set his cup down, nodded to

Joe and they went outside. Over a brief silence, Sherill was watching Jean and saw her glance go to the room's inner door. Tears came to her eyes and she turned quickly away, asking, "More coffee?"

He let her fill his cup and she at once turned back to the stove. With her back to him, she tried to hide the gesture of lifting a hand to her eyes. And he sensed her utter loneliness and despair in that moment and told her:

"Don't keep holding it back, Jean."

She stood there without speaking, her shoulders barely moving as she held back her sobs. Then abruptly she faced around, unashamedly letting him see the tears that glistened along her cheeks. Somehow she managed a smile.

"I can hear Brick saying, 'Stop your blubberin', youngster,' " she said. "I always listened to him and now, you see, I'm remembering. Once he was a top hand, the best man who ever worked for dad. He was fine and proud, beautiful to watch on a horse. When I was little, he used to take me for rides ahead of him on his saddle and I think I've loved him ever since. When that loco horse crippled him, dad wanted to buy him a saddle shop in town. He wouldn't take it, said he wanted to stay with us. So dad paid him top-hand wages and even after dad died he stayed on. He was probably the best friend I ever had."

She paused as the sound of thunder suddenly rumbled in from the north. And now the wind was dying out and the drumming of the rain on the roof was settling to a steady low undertone.

Sherill saw that it was helping her to talk. She was getting herself in hand. He helped her along by drawling, "I should have known Brick."

She smiled faintly at some thought. "You should," she said. "For some reason he seemed to think you were the one to go to about the Major."

"He didn't like Donovan?"

"He hated him!" she breathed, and he noticed that her fists were tightly clenched. "It's my fault that the Major didn't leave long ago."

"Nothing's your fault. Get over thinkin' that. Brick would tell you the same thing."

She stood there thinking about that. She looked up at him, softly saying, "I want to believe that," and he could see the beginning of that belief in her eyes.

"You can. These things just happen. Brick didn't strike me as the kind that would ever want a long white beard. He had his fun and maybe he was beginning to think the fun was over. Which is the time to call it quits."

She gave him an odd look that was a blend of tenderness and warmth. "Jim Sherill, there's something about you I — "

He wasn't to know the completion of her thought, although many times afterward he remembered her words and tried to puzzle out their unspoken ending. For just then the sound of horses moving around back of the house came to them and Jean broke off and turned to the door.

A moment later Phil Rust came in, water streaming from his slicker, and the moment that had brought them so close to each other had passed.

Rust said, "All set. I'm takin' Joe's mare along to pack our possibles on, Jean. If you don't mind drivin', Joe's cleaning up the buggy and rigging the tarp so's you won't get wet. He'll come along behind you in the buckboard. Better get started. It's late."

Sherill went into the living room and, with a last look at Brick, took his slicker from the chair where Jean had laid it. He put it on in the kitchen and as he was buckling it, Jean told him, "You must come back, Jim. Soon."

He nodded, his glance openly clinging to

her. He wanted to remember this smile she was giving him.

He turned away finally and went out into the rain.

By the lamplight shining from the door, he made out the horses and found his saddle on a big sorrel. He wiped the water from the saddle before he mounted and then Phil Rust came over and handed him a lead rope. Presently they swung out across the yard and into the cotton-woods, Rust leading the other pair of horses.

Sherill turned and had a final glimpse of Jean's slender shape silhouetted in the door's lighted rectangle. She lifted a hand to them just before the trees hid her from sight and then he was listening to Rust's impatient cursing at the lagging of the lead-horses.

They rode side by side as they took the slope behind the corral, looking back down on the faint glow of light coming from the open maw of the barn. Phil Rust laughed softly, saying, "Joe tried to hand me half a month's pay to swap places with him. Damned if I would!"

Sherill's mind was running ahead now and he thought of something that made him say, "We're short on rifles. Could we go back for a couple?"

"There's three forty-fours packed under the tarp on that paint you've got hold of," Phil Rust told him, and from then on Sherill began to respect this good-natured and slat-bodied young 'puncher.

They rode slowly, Phil's lead animals now and then balking. He swore at them mildly and persuaded them on with a practiced patience, and twenty minutes later they rode in on the charred mound of the shack, the corral and a feebly burning fire to find Mitch and Jake squatting near the blaze wrapped in their slickers.

No word was said beyond their first casual greeting and they at once started saddling, Mitch and Jake automatically accepting the fact that they were going to be on the move. Jake picked the brown horse and Mitch threw his saddle on the chunkier paint.

Jake, the last to be ready, was lashing his blanketroll behind the cantle before he broke the rain-droning silence, asking, "Where we headed?"

"We'll have to talk it over," Sherill told him. He sauntered over to the fire and they followed. Shortly he said, "Ed being back means that Purdy probably went up after him last night."

"He must've," Jake put in. "At least he was there with the rest this afternoon."

232

"Then he must know his way around in those hills to the north," Sherill mused. "It's a good bet that Donovan will be with them. If I was Donovan and had sixty head of horses and a bunch of steers to play with, I'd run the horses on through fast and mess up their sign with the beef."

"He picked a sweet night for hidin' sign," Mitch interrupted dryly.

"He did, and he'll play it for all it's worth. He'll drive right on past their layout and deep into the hills. He's got the pick of three ways to go, north, east or west. My hunch is he'll head north. Or," he added tiredly, "maybe after tonight we'd better not play my hunches."

"The hell we don't!" Jake bridled. "You forget what happened tonight, Jim. I was so sure nothing'd happen that I left Mitch here alone and went on that sashay after Donovan. We all make mistakes."

"Sure," Mitch agreed. "Go ahead with your hunch."

Sherill felt somewhat relieved as he went on: "Then here it is. Ed would have told me if they'd ever driven horses east or west. He didn't mention it. But we did talk of workin' horses north through Canada. Mitch knows they've already run some up that way."

"Not many. But a few," Mitch said.

"Which means that Donovan, with Purdy's help, will probably try to make a quick drive all the way through to some spot near the border. He'll hole up there and sell a few head here and there as he gets the chance. How does it sound?"

"Like sense," Jake drawled. Both Mitch and Phil Rust nodded agreement.

"There'll be two or three of their crew draggin' that beef along as fast as they can behind the horses," Sherill went on. "Last night it took us five hours to bring the herd out. They'll be at least that long taking it back as far as their layout. So by daylight we could be ahead of them if Jake can show us the way."

Jake said, "You could do that without me showin' you."

"Look, Jim," Mitch cut in worriedly, "it's all right to get ahead of 'em. But what good'll it do us? There's four of us. Count out Ed, and maybe Slim and at least one man Jake took care of tonight. Throw in Donovan and there's still six of the crew left. We might pick off a couple. Even so, where would it get us?"

"It might get us somewhere if we picked our spot."

"But where?"

"Remember the box you ran me into?" Sherill asked.

A slow grin came to Mitch's face as he thought that over. "Not bad," he drawled.

"Which box?" Jake wanted to know.

"I heard Mitch call it Six Mile Canyon. It drops down onto a low pass that runs between two straight-up hills. You think this canyon's an easy way up out of the pass and then you wind up smack against a wall it'd take a crow half a day to fly over."

"There's a way out," Mitch said. "The way we took you out."

"One man could fort up at the head of that trail and make another last stand for George Custer," Sherill countered. "Forget that trail."

"Maybe I know the place," Jake said thoughtfully. "Twelve, fifteen miles above that meadow? A high overhang on the peak to the east?"

"That's it," Mitch said.

"Can you take us there, Jake? Without them seein' us or cutting in ahead to give away what we're doin'?" Sherill asked.

"I could try," Jake said in a way that eased Sherill's worry.

"Then let's get started," Sherill said, and turned out to his horse.

★ ★ ★

235

★ ★ ★

Caleb Donovan headed straight for the river when he left Anchor's corral. He didn't even look back to be sure Brick was down. There was no need to look. He had seen the bullet strike.

He didn't ride fast, knowing that the darkness and the noise of the wind and rain hid him. He was wholly engrossed in considering how his leaving Anchor this suddenly would change things, for he had this afternoon told Ed and Purdy what to do with the herd, had planned on joining them within a week. As it had turned out, he would be with them before morning.

The river was somewhere close ahead when he suddenly remembered George Lovelace. He pulled the bay into a halt and sat there thinking about Lovelace, about time and distance and how much he could demand of a horse. In the end his decision was made and, brutally, he threw the spurs into the bay and headed for the Whitewater road.

That first fright held the bay to a hard run for better than two miles. When the animal began lagging, the Major used the spur again.

He rode the foundered animal along the town's muddy street at ten-thirty, turning in at Kramer's livery and changing his saddle to a short-coupled Anchor claybank he had

236

brought in last week to be sold. The claybank was hard-mouthed and as Donovan left the lot he used the bit viciously in quieting the animal down out of his eagerness to go.

At the *River House* Donovan learned that George Lovelace was on his boat, which was going down-river at daylight. *Just like him,* was the Major's thought when he considered the proposition Lovelace had made him in the light of the man's departure.

He tied the claybank in under a warehouse's overhang and trudged out across the levee toward the *Queen*'s lights shining through the blur of the rain. From one of the deck hands he learned that Lovelace was still up and about. Above, the darkness of the long stretch of hurricane deck was broken by pale light shining from one of the saloon windows. Through that window Donovan looked in on George Lovelace and his pilot seated at a small table in one corner of the big room. The two men were studying a chart of the river.

The Major's entry brought Lovelace's head up and he peered into the gloom that shadowed the door, not recognizing Donovan's bulky shape and tartly asking, "Who is it? We're busy."

"Just me, Commodore," Donovan answered. He walked across to the table, his slicker trailing a thin line of wetness along the carpet. He looked down at Lovelace, "There's something I'd like to talk over with you. Outside."

Lovelace gave him an irritable glance, yet immediately arose from the table, telling his pilot, "Won't be a minute, John." He led the way across the saloon to a door on the riverward side and went out, Donovan following.

"You shouldn't be seeing me here," Lovelace snapped in a low voice as they crossed to the rail.

"It's either here or no place at all," the Major replied. "I hear you pull out in the mornin'."

Anticipating what Donovan was about to say, Lovelace said, "I've written a letter that was going in the mail to you in the morning, Captain."

"What does it say?"

"What we talked over is no longer necessary. I've decided not to go through with it."

"That's a shame."

Donovan's tone made Lovelace peer at him closely. "Why?"

"Because Sherill brought his horses down out of the hills this morning. Because tonight I had a crew drive the herd off again."

Lovelace's eyes opened wide in startlement. Then, in some anger, he said, "You should have consulted me first."

"Should I? Was that the agreement?" Donovan held out a hand. "Where's the thousand?"

Lovelace backed away a step. "My reasons for making that offer no longer exist, Captain," he said.

"But it's finished, done with," Donovan drawled in a deceptively mild way. "So I've earned the thousand. Get it."

A sudden gust of rain swept the deck and Lovelace edged over toward the saloon door, saying in his pompous way, "It's unfortunate that you were so hasty. However, there's nothing I can do about it."

"There's something I can do," Donovan said. "The sheriff might like to hear what I have to say."

A smirk crossed Lovelace's round face. "Your word against mine, Captain?" He laughed. "Don't forget what happened before you left the Army."

Donovan's temper had risen over these moments. But his anger was focused upon the circumstances that had defeated him rather than upon the Commodore. He hadn't expected his threat of going to the law to have much effect and he had made it only for the reason of wanting to see what

Lovelace's reaction would be. He had read that reaction so rightly, the Commodore's confidence was so invulnerable, that he felt foolish now over having thought he had a chance for that thousand. If Lovelace hadn't used this trick of going back on his word he would have found some other way.

Donovan understood the Commodore's dishonesty only because his own mind worked in much the same way. And because of his realization that they were pretty much two of a kind, respecting Lovelace not at all, he now acted with violence.

He stepped in on Lovelace, reached out and shoved him hard on one shoulder. Lovelace spun around, crying out in fright. Donovan clutched him by the coat collar with one hand, by the seat of the pants with the other, and pushed him toward the rail. Lovelace was falling forward, half running, when Donovan with a mighty heave lifted him clear of the deck and out across the rail.

Lovelace's hoarse scream was prolonged and agonized and ended suddenly with a loud splash that echoed across the sound of the rain.

The shadows of the foredeck had swallowed Donovan's shapeless form by the time the saloon door burst open and the Commodore's pilot appeared. The confusion and the shouting along the boiler-deck was such that Donovan wasn't even seen as he walked the stage to the levee. He heard a splash as someone dived after Lovelace and once he caught the Commodore's voice calling for help. He was smiling in a way he seldom did as he swung up onto the claybank and turned upstreet. And he was thinking, *It was worth the ride, damned if it wasn't.*

Once clear of the town, he headed down-river toward the high-country. He was punishing the claybank in much the same way he had the bay on the way in.

Dawn found them pushing steadily up through the higher foothills, and with the strengthening of that first gray light the breeze drifting down off the cloud-shrouded peaks brought them occasional flurries of snow. It was bitterly cold and they were constantly breathing into their stiff cupped hands, their exhalations trailing out in a misty vapor behind them. Now and then there were a few patches of slushy snow about them and they could look ahead and above and see the snow getting whiter.

Jake finally asked, "Anyone bring an axe?"

"Sure," Phil Rust told him. "Why?"

"Someone's goin' to have to chop me out of my hull."

"Let's have breakfast," Sherill said, reining the big sorrel off into a thick stand of blue spruce.

They built a fire and fed their animals some grain and Jake mixed a batch of pan-bread. Phil's pack produced a slab from a quarter of beef and they cut steaks and pan-fried them over the hot coals. They didn't really stop shaking from the cold until they had washed down the biscuits and steak with coffee.

Mitch was showing the effects of having gone two nights without rest. His eyes were red and heavy-lidded and for the first time Sherill noticed he moved with effort, tiredly. Sherill himself had given way to his weariness during the night, dozing from time to time. His snatches of sleep had done him little good, however, for his eyes still had that gritty feeling of having been open too long and his leg-muscles ached from the strain of all this saddle-work.

Now the meal revived him considerably, as it seemed to be putting new strength in Mitch. Once he was warm Sherill relished the piney fragrance of the air and the look of the dripping pines and these rarer lofty spruce, reminded of late-fall elk hunts with

Ned in the high-country above the Yellow-stone.

Strangely, this reminder of Ned didn't make him uneasy. Last night's awesome turn of bad luck had stripped him for a time of all emotion except for certain new and deeply-satisfying thoughts of Jean. Last night after the shots had died away, there hadn't seemed much he could lose. Now his feelings for Jean somehow made up for the other things and he could look back upon yesterday and the night before without the rancour coming alive in him. He could think of Ruth and Ned and tell himself, *They were two of a kind, not my kind* and halfway begin to believe it.

This ride in for a last try at the horses had lost all semblance of a meaning to him beyond its being a game, a matching of his wits against Caleb Donovan, whom he hated with all the passion he had so bewilderingly tried to focus on Ruth and Ned.

The Major was a cleaner, surer target for his feelings than the two friends he had lost. There was nothing about Donovan he could remember with respect. His feelings for the man were definite, black against white, backed by the knowledge of Donovan's cal-lousness toward Jean and of his having destroyed a man incapable of defending himself simply to satisfy a cold, killing urge.

Sherill had planned his moves carefully so far and now he was trying to think ahead as he asked Jake, "How far to go?"

"Ten bad miles maybe, if we don't run any chances. Seven easier ones if we do."

Sherill thought a moment, trying to judge how far the horses could have been driven during these eight hours. At length he looked at Mitch, asking, "How's that country above the meadow? I didn't see much of it on the way down."

"Not easy," Mitch said. "They'd have to string out along some of the washes. And there's rock, slow goin'."

"Then we take the long way, Jake," Sherill said.

They cleaned their pans, Phil threw his diamond-hitch on the lead-horse again and they rode on into the cold drizzle.

Better than an hour later the rain turned definitely to a light snow and they were riding in a cloud, a ghostly grayness all about them with the snow gently falling and the air very still. Sherill began wondering if Jake knew his bearings. But the wolfer kept steadily on. They were making good time.

They rounded the shoulder of a peak lost in the clouds, then dipped down across a high valley and climbed again. The clouds finally thinned until Sherill could make out the faint glow of the sun. He saw that they were travelling east now and he knew that Jake must be making the wide swing to bring them in on the pass from the north.

Now that the rain was behind them they could keep reasonably warm. They stopped twice in the next three hours and built fires and finally they were warm enough to keep on going with no thought of stopping.

The clouds suddenly broke away from around them as they climbed, and then they were riding in warm sunlight across an undulating snowfield of blinding brightness. They had swung into the south and above them towered the bulk of a low peak. It was, Sherill judged, close to ten o'clock.

He pulled on past Mitch and in behind Jake, asking, "We're close?"

"Another mile," the wolfer answered.

"I'm going up there for a look, Jake."

"Up where?" Jake asked, turning around.

Sherill nodded to the east shoulder of the mountain, saying, "If it's clearing below, we may get a look at 'em."

"Why don't we all go take a look?" Jake said promptly, and turned his horse up the slope.

It took them a full quarter-hour of back-and-forth climbing to bring that low-country to the south into view. And when they finally looked down upon it, the labored blowing of their horses breaking the stillness, they were keenly disappointed.

To the east and close below lay the pass. Why he had ridden up Six Mile Canyon his first time through here was plainer than ever to Sherill now that he could see it. This slope on which they stood fell abruptly to the level of the pass. Directly opposite a higher peak flanked the pass sheerly with the overhang Jake had mentioned jutting out high above.

Six Mile Canyon swung climbing toward the east along the foot of this peak opposite, finally to become a part of it, a deep notch in one of its low shoulders. Southward, the pass emptied into gradually falling ground that broke up into the outspread fingers of washes and deep canyons.

Their disappointment came from the fact that, below the pass, all that lower country lay shrouded in gray cloud.

Mitch said, "Hell, all this work for nothin'. I'd like me a nice warm bed and a pint of red-eye right now."

Sherill was still looking downward, although the rest had finished with that and were waiting for him. He sat there for better than a minute, his glance not moving.

Then abruptly he said, "Take a look down there now, Jake."

The wolfer's head came around and he squinted against the sun's glare, saying after a long look, "It's breakin' up some."

"We'll sit it out," Sherill said, swinging stiffly aground.

He loosened his cinch, dropped the reins and walked over to lean against a hip-high boulder. He opened his slicker and took out tobacco and rolled up a smoke and then the others followed suit, getting down and stretching, Mitch yawning loudly.

Mitch came over to Sherill and held out a hand for the tobacco, asking, "What're you expectin'?"

"Can't tell yet. But there's plenty of time."

Mitch concentrated on manipulating his cold-stiffened fingers. "You're pretty sure about the time. How come?"

"Take a look down there now."

Mitch did, his look puzzled. "What?"

"Down where the cloud's gone away from the side of that second knob. In the canyon below it."

Mitch looked again. Suddenly he grinned, saying, "So we have our fun after all."

"We do," Sherill said.

And Mitch looked again, seeing that dark snaking line at the bottom of the canyon slowly twisting, changing shape as it climbed toward the pass.

There were Sherill's horses.

VII

That morning Caleb Donovan carried his breakfast outside and in under the cookhouse lean-to out of the rain, sitting at the lower end of the stack of split pine and eating quickly as he looked off through the dawn-lighted pines past the barn and to the bottom of the meadow. Off there the horses were moving on up out of sight through the steady drizzle, the bell-mare's bell sounding faintly from the upper distance. Two men who hadn't yet eaten were working the herd. Bill Purdy and Slim, who had done the cooking, were inside. The remaining two crewmen were still several miles below, pushing Anchor's cattle along the line the horses had taken.

Donovan just now heard the ring of big-rowelled spurs and a moment later Bill Purdy walked in under the lean-to. He squatted down near Donovan, asking, "What'll we do about Slim? He can barely walk."

"Swap him for the kid. Put him with the beef. We need Ted with the horses anyway."

Purdy frowned, not liking this. "Slim's

had a belly-full of Sherill. Suppose he decides to drift?"

"Put Horse with the beef, too. Have him keep an eye on Slim."

"I don't like it, Major."

Donovan smiled as much as he ever did, "Why worry? We couldn't want it better than it is. What if we lose the cattle? All we're doing with 'em is running a bluff."

"That Sherill. He's a hard-headed devil."

"We can forget Sherill."

Purdy seemed to doubt that but didn't say so.

Donovan went on eating, idly wondering about Sherill. He wasn't really expecting any complications, sure that he had spread enough confusion around Anchor last night to discourage everyone concerned. Last night he had been with Ed Stedman off there beyond the line-shack and had personally seen to it that Sherill and whoever was with him were set afoot. He had felt about the same degree of emotion in deliberately shooting the two horses as he had later in just as deliberately killing Brick Chase.

Seeing Ed Stedman cut down had been a different thing entirely. He had been furious, blaming Ed for taking a stupid chance, for drifting in toward the burning shack and exposing himself on the hunch that he might get a shot at Sherill. Stupidity was something the Major could never forgive in a man and not until hours afterward, looking back on it, had he finally been grateful that Ed was out of the way. Sherill, or one of his men, had saved him a distasteful chore; for Ed had definitely outlived his usefulness.

Such was his cold-blooded reasoning now as he glanced at Bill Purdy. Here was a more straightforward matter. Purdy was a killer and expected little beyond fair wages and a reasonable amount of protection from the law. He could handle the crew, or what was left of it.

Although none of the crew had known Donovan until yesterday, he had known them through his dealings with Ed. Now he briefly considered them, judging how much he could demand of each. Slim was crippled, therefore a nonentity. The old man known simply as Horse — wanted by Wells-Fargo for a small part in a stage holdup — was too mild and ineffectual to be of much use in a tight spot. Therefore these two were the logical ones to leave in charge of Anchor's cattle. Young Ted Fawley, the wrangler, Idaho Gaines, Charley Baker and Boyd Green all had their good reasons for being up here and, because of those reasons, would fight if it came to a showdown. They would be with the horse-herd.

Now Donovan swallowed the last of his coffee and tossed the tin plate and the cup over onto the sodden mound of the ash-heap, discarding them in the knowledge he would never again be back here.

He reached in under the slicker and his sheepskin coat for a toothpick and sat there running its point between his big solid teeth, his expression wholly sober as he listened to the drone of the rain and looked out through the dripping pines, deliberately thinking of his plan.

Shortly he told Purdy, "This rain'll last all day, maybe into the night. We hit it about right."

"What do I tell Slim to do with the Anchor stuff?"

"He's to keep right on our tails until late this afternoon. Then he can swing east for a couple hours, lay over tonight and push on tomorrow. If he can spot a likely place late tomorrow, he can turn the herd loose."

"Just forget it, eh?"

"Maybe. Maybe not. We'll do fifty miles today, another fifty tomorrow. The next day you and a couple of the others can come back, look things over and bring the beef on if you find everything clear. But the main idea is for Slim and Horse to follow us until we're high in that rocky going, high enough not to have to worry too much about sign."

"What do we do with the horses once we're up there?"

"Sell 'em in small bunches. If we find the right place, we can work things up there like Sherill wanted to." Donovan stood up and buckled his slicker, adding, "It could be a good thing that Sherill came along. We needed someone to push us into this thing. You all set to go?"

Purdy nodded. "I'll go see Slim." He walked around the corner of the shack and out of sight.

Ten minutes later they were riding out from the small corral into the foot of the meadow and a quarter-hour later caught up with the drag of the herd in the timber beyond the meadow's upper end. Purdy stayed behind to relieve Boyd Green while Donovan went on through the alders along the herd's right flank. Presently he came up with Gaines, leading the bell-mare, and told him, "Go on back and eat, Idaho. The stuff's hot." He took the lead-rope from him.

It was no time at all before the Major became impatient at the mare's plodding gait. He took a couple of turns with the rope around his hand, pulling her along faster.

She fought the rope for a few minutes, then simply let Donovan drag her along. Finally he saw the futility of trying to persuade her and slowed the pace and she settled right back into her easy jog.

The mare, he realized, must have formed her travelling habits on Sherill's drive up to this country and, thus reminded of the man, he was mildly angry with himself for not having known who Sherill was days ago. Being a man of devious ways, Donovan could now grudgingly admire Sherill's downright audacity in trying what he had. *And damn near getting away with it,* he added. He had been completely deceived by Sherill and he knew now that nothing but freakish luck had swung the situation around in his favor.

Forty minutes after he had relieved Gaines, Purdy came along and showed him a turning up along a rocky gulch that led to a broad ledge along the shoulder of a bald low peak, telling him, "We're makin' for a pass up there."

Donovan nodded. "We could move faster if this mare would wake up."

Purdy looked back at the mare, shrugging and drawling, "Back behind it seems fast enough."

So Donovan was satisfied. They were striking patches of snow now and light snow-flurries were mixed in with the rain and it was bitterly cold. They worked down off the ledge into a deep canyon and Purdy went on ahead and out of sight and some twenty minutes later Donovan came up on a fire, Purdy standing by it.

Purdy rode out from the fire saying, "I'll spell you while you thaw out," and Donovan surrendered the lead-rope.

He stood there by the fire holding his slicker open so that it would catch the heat and, as the uneven column of horses trotted past, a warm feeling of satisfaction settled through him. These were fine animals, all sound and of a matching bigness, their colors solid. They were as good a string of animals as he had ever seen on a cavalry post and for a second time that morning he paid Sherill a small tribute of respect in admiring them.

Idaho Gaines came up, dropped off near the fire and sauntered over briskly rubbing his hands, drawling, "God, it's cold. But better than bein' wet," and Donovan only then realized that the rain had stopped and that the gray light was thinning.

Looking skyward, he could see patches of blue through white fleecy cloud. Off to the north the clouds had fallen away and it was clear. He could see the high crest of two peaks off there. The look of the weather at once worried him.

"We could use some rain," he told Gaines.

His crewman smiled ruefully. "Don't think we won't get it. Two hours from now we'll either be soaked to the skin or drifted over with snow."

"What makes you so sure?"

"I been livin' here too long not to know."

Gaines was right. Long before that two hours had passed, the clouds closed down on them and they were riding up on the pass in a blinding snow-storm feeling their way along a margin of timber. Through the trees they now and then sighted the deep chasm of Six Mile Canyon dropping away to their right.

Purdy and Donovan were together now, working the drag, with the horses up ahead sometimes out of sight in the smother of snow. They rode down-headed and with shoulders hunched.

Donovan was feeling good, so good that he reined in close to Purdy, saying, "This'll fix it. No one's going to follow us through here."

Purdy nodded. "Not bad."

To their left a steep slope of broken granite climbed into the white swirling nothingness. It was from up there that a rifleshot slapped suddenly down at them, the unexpectedness of the sound bringing Donovan's head around in an uncomprehending stare.

Above him, only ten feet away, Purdy's head dropped forward as though he was about to pray. Then Purdy slowly toppled sideways, his horse shying and throwing him. After staring unbelievingly an instant, Donovan raked his horse's flanks with spurs.

He felt the air-whip of a second bullet and heard the brittle explosion of the shot as his animal lunged into a run. Now the trees suddenly loomed out of the obscurity and Donovan swung right and let the horse run into them, his massive body rigid in expectation of a bullet slamming into his back.

A branch raked across the face, the horse jinked around a thicket of oak, nearly throwing him, and directly afterward the animal swung sharply left, coming within two yards of the rim's drop-off. Donovan had a brief glimpse of the canyon-bottom lying only fifty feet below as he used the rein-ends to send the horse back up through the timber.

Close ahead sounded the hollow explosion of a Colt's. And now Donovan reached inside his slicker and drew his forty-five. He was suddenly clear of the trees and racing along behind the galloping animals at the drag of the herd.

Purdy's horse ran down off the slope and past Donovan, stirrups swinging crazily from the empty saddle, and from behind him and up the slope the rifle that had dropped Purdy was sending down methodical sharp echoes that sounded over the hoof-thunder of the stampeded horses. More shots came from up ahead and Donovan reined back into the cover of the pine, reaching up now to wipe the snow from his face.

Suddenly he came to the rim of the canyon again and, close ahead, saw the horses breaking through the trees and pounding into the head of the canyon, turning back below him. He looked down, saw only a steep talus slope dropping to the canyon-bottom. He put his horse down along it.

Once below, he ran several hundred yards and then pulled in, hearing no shots now, watching the horses run past him in bunches of three and four. Idaho Gaines abruptly appeared out of the snow-fog, coming in on him at a hard run.

Gaines' eyes were wide with excitement as he asked, "What happened to Purdy?"

"They got him."

A look Donovan didn't like crossed the 'puncher's face. There was strong fear in his eyes as he blurted out, "Charley's cashed in, too. What the hell we goin' to do?"

"Follow this canyon on out and lose our-
selves," Donovan told him levelly, a hard
glitter of anger in his glance. "Where's your
guts, man? We're still all right."

"Like hell we are! This is Six Mile. It's
a box, and if we get out we go the way
we came in."

The last of the horses had streaked out
of sight into the tall pines half-blocking the
canyon mouth and now, as the hoof-pound
of the running herd became muted and then
died out altogether, Sherill looked across at
Jake lying behind a boulder ten yards away,
the .44 still against his cheek. The wolfer
had taken off his slicker and his buckskin-clad
shape was solidly sifted over so that he
blended into the snow and was hard to see.

The snow was coming straight down, laying
a barely audible whisper of sound against
the heavy stillness. It had already covered
the sprawled figure Sherill could vaguely see
lying a hundred yards below near the trees
in the mouth of the canyon. Charley Baker
had been leading the bell-mare and Sherill
could still feel the regret of having watched
him fall before Jake's first bullet, impossible
though the shot had seemed as his ghostly
shadow moved behind the white curtain in
the obscure distance.

He hadn't seen either of the other two riders he had briefly glimpsed go down. He hadn't used his carbine, choosing the Colt's instead and throwing his shots against boulders ahead of the herd so that the noise of the ricochets and of the shots themselves would turn the animals up the canyon.

Now he came stiffly erect and walked over to Jake, warily glancing below as he moved. He said, "I'll get on down there and you can bring the horses along." He wanted to be sure of this, wanted to seal the mouth of the canyon so effectively that he would have Donovan really trapped.

Rising, Jake said, "Someone's movin' off there."

The wolfer was looking in the direction out of which the horse-herd had come and now abruptly rocked the Winchester to his shoulder. Then he slowly lowered it, drawling, "Mitch."

Mitch Lockwood walked his horse up to them every few moments glancing back over his shoulder. He stopped close below Sherill, asking, "Did it come off?"

Sherill nodded, seeing that the tension of a strong excitement had eased the tiredness from Mitch's face.

"That fool Rust," Mitch complained mildly. "We had a clear chance at Purdy and Donovan. Phil was layin' alongside me sort of prayin' that he could blow Donovan in two. I had Purdy in my sights, thinkin' I'd wing him. Then all of a sudden Rust opens up right as Purdy swings in line with Donovan and damned if he doesn't hit Purdy dead center."

"What about the Major?" Sherill asked.

Mitch shook his head. "He made some fast tracks. We lost him. Phil's got some choice words I'll have to learn."

Sherill tilted his head toward the lower trees. "Let's wind this up and build a fire." He started on past Mitch's horse, thought of something and asked, "Phil's at the head of that trail?"

"Not yet, but he will be soon."

In the next hour they got a fire going well back in the timber from the canyon-mouth and took turns warming themselves. The canyon's outlet into the pass was a scant two hundred yards across. Jake picked the pine-clump on the far side, directly under the sheer-rising shoulder of the peak, at the point from which he would watch. Opposite him, Mitch finally made himself comfortable between two big boulders on the rim so that he could look out and down, seeing everything there was to see the breadth of the canyon.

Sherill stayed with Mitch a few minutes before giving way to his restlessness and abruptly announcing, "I'll have a look-see." He mounted the sorrel and headed out along the run.

He couldn't see much after the first mile, the depth of the canyon gradually becoming obscured by the unchanging curtain of the snow. Finally he gave it up and turned back and rode that mile even more carefully than on coming up. He saw nothing move down there, not an animal or a man; nor did he see the flicker of a fire.

When he came back down to Mitch, he drawled, "They're out of sight. We'll sit tight and see what happens."

At this same moment Caleb Donovan, hugging a fire some distance up the canyon, was listening to his men arguing and getting no help from them. Boyd Green, in his slow way, was insisting that they could wait until dark, then make a break for it or sneak down out of the mouth of the canyon and past whoever had laid the ambush.

"Boyd, you're loco," young Ted Fawley told him. "You could stand with your back against one wall and come awful close to ropin' a horse against the other. Man, they could even throw rocks and hit us, it's so narrow."

None of them were ever to know that there was a way out of the canyon along that deer-trail. The knowledge had died with Bill Purdy, the only one of them who had ever ridden it.

The Major was thankful that Idaho Gaines wasn't here. He had sent Gaines down below better than an hour ago to stop anyone coming up the canyon. Gaines was opinionated, he'd been badly frightened and he'd be no help now.

Up there along the pass just before that sudden violence struck them, Caleb Donovan had been thinking of something that had considerable possibilities. Why, he had been asking himself, couldn't this string of horses be driven east and over into Dakota Territory as soon as they'd made good their getaway? Every brand had been reworked and at that distance the chances were remote that any animal would ever be recognized. Why, then, couldn't he set himself up a legitimate business near some cavalry post and, using Boyd Green or Ted Fawley, sell directly to the Army and collect a hundred and a quarter an animal instead of the usual forty or fifty?

All that was changed now. The herd had been driven above along the canyon and would probably be left there. He and the others stood maybe a fifty-fifty chance of getting out of here alive if, as he was fairly certain, it was Sherill who had run them up into this box. From what the others had said, at least three men had opened up on them. Possibly more. But even three men with rifles could keep ten times their number from breaking out of the narrow foot of the canyon and down off the pass.

So he could forget the Dakota idea.

Wait! he told himself, *Maybe not!*

And before the thought that had struck him took on its final form he swung around on Boyd Green, saying in a clipped voice, "Shut up and listen."

Green's startled glance came up to him and Ted Fawley, reading the urgency in his tone, checked himself on interrupting what Green had been saying.

"We're fools to be wasting time here," Donovan went on after a moment's hesitation. He held out his hand, letting the snowflakes settle on it. "We can see sixty yards, seventy at the most through this stuff. And they can't see any better than we can. Our best chance is to make a run for it right now."

"Night's better," Green insisted stubbornly.

"It is unless they build fires. Which they will," Donovan said. "Remember, this Sherill's no fool."

"We know that," Ted Fawley said. "Go on with what you were sayin'."

"If they're waiting at the foot of this cut, they can see us for maybe five seconds as we go past. Once — "

"And knock us down like chickens on a roost," Green cut in.

"Not if we run the herd through with us," Donovan said evenly.

He saw them glance at each other, saw a new interest come alive in each man's eyes.

"We'll mix in through the bunch and drive through fast," he went on. "Once we're clear, we'll never give them another chance to crowd us into a spot like this."

Ted Fawley, looking at Green, slowly grinned and drawled, "How about it, Boyd?"

Green nodded, not without a certain reluctance. "It could work."

Donovan said, "You two go up and work around the herd. Take the bell off the mare. Push 'em on down slow and I'll get Gaines and we'll fall in with the leaders. Remember that big burned stick we passed on the way up?"

They both nodded at his mention of a long lightning-blasted pine that stood in almost the exact center of the canyon half a mile or so below.

"When you hit that, start making your

run for it. Don't use your guns but make those horses run. Go right on through with them."

"While you go first," Green said dryly.

"Would you rather go through ahead?" Donovan asked.

Green thought about it, finally shrugged and said, "I'll stay where you put me."

Without another word, Donovan turned and walked back into the trees to the horses. As he was leaving the trees, Fawley and Green rode the opposite way.

Down below, Idaho Gaines didn't like the plan at all. He was still jumpy, badly scared. So Donovan told him flatly, "Either you go with us or you stay. Take your pick."

Gaines thought it over for several minutes, until they caught the sound of the herd coming along above. Then he said quickly, "I'll side you," and they reined on out, looking off through the snow trying to see the herd approaching.

Now, abruptly, the lead animals trotted in out of the snow-fog and went on past. Donovan said, "Let a few more go," and another bunch of seven horses drifted past along the far wall, barely in sight.

Then a dark mass of animals moved up out of the obscurity and Donovan reined out and along with them. He called back to

Gaines, "Not too close to me," and Gaines fell back a little.

A tension gathered in Donovan and he was excited in the same way he had been five years ago when, summoned to his commanding officer's quarters, he hadn't known whether the decision was to be a court-martial or an accepted resignation. There was that same feeling of desperation in him now as there had been then, although he coldly failed to recognize it and kept telling himself that all the odds were in his favor.

Something else he wouldn't recognize was the small paralysis of surprise that still remained in him at the unexpectedness of this thing. It angered him to think that Sherill had outguessed him and as he rode on now, eyes squinted against the light pelting of the snow, he was hating the man with more passion than he was normally capable of feeling toward any man or any thing.

Sherill was responsible for all this, for his having been discovered, for his losing his security at Anchor, now for losing this sizeable stake in horses. He had the warming thought that possibly, just possibly, he might get a shot at Sherill on the way out.

So now he made his careful preparations. He unbuckled the slicker and took it off and cast it aside. He was fairly warm, since last night he had thought to put on his sheepskin coat before leaving Anchor. He drew the Colt's from under the coat in the same way he had drawn it last night under his slicker before shooting Brick, his hand moving furtively although there was no need for that now. He checked the weapon. As an afterthought, he dropped a sixth shell into the empty chamber he normally kept under the hammer. He might need that extra one.

He dropped the Colt's into the broad pocket of the sheepskin and, letting his horse drift along at a trot with the bunch, sat rubbing his hands, warming them, wanting them to be limber. He swallowed with difficulty, clearing his throat that was tight with anticipation. He told himself he wasn't afraid. He never had known fear as other men know it, consciously. But he was as close to knowing it now as he had ever been.

He thought of one more thing. Across the pommel of his saddle, a Whitman, ran a heavy coat strap. He inspected it, running his hand in under it and pulling against it with a lot of strength. It held.

The horses broke around the lightning-blasted pine and suddenly Donovan heard the steady drumming of hooves behind him lift to a quicker beat. Then the big animals alongside were trotting faster. He reined on over and into the bunch and his horse, feeling the excitement, broke into a run when the others did.

He quickly ran the reins in under the saddle's coat strap, his hands strangely trembling. He looked ahead and saw the rim to the left falling away. The thunder of hooves was all around him now, building to a loud crescendo. The horses to either side shied away, then were crowded in again by those beyond. His horse was running free.

He thrust his hand through the coat strap, taking a tight hold. He drew the Colt's. Then, lifting left boot from stirrup, he hunched his big body far forward and to the right. His left shoulder and chest were against the horse's heaving shoulder, all his weight against the strap and the one stirrup.

Sherill was with Mitch when he caught that first far-off murmur of the herd running down along the canyon. He said, "This'll be it," and he and Mitch ran for their horses, pulling off their slickers and dropping them.

They ran their horses along the rim and Sherill looked back and down and saw the herd break through the smother of snow, the lead-animals running hard, stampeding, ears back, manes and tails flying.

He came on down where the rim dropped

onto the pass and rounded the last clump of trees and drew his Colt's as the leaders pounded past. He couldn't see the trees where Jake waited across the way, so thick was the fall of snow. Reining in, he looked back along the heaving mass of the running horses trying to pick out a rider's outline. Then from across the mouth of the canyon Jake's rifle suddenly cracked above the roar.

At the same instant he saw the saddle bay horse, saw the leg hooked over the saddle, saw the flat sole of Donovan's boot cocked straight out at him.

The bay was well over toward Jake's side, nearly out of the mouth of the canyon now.

Sherill raked the big sorrel with spurs and the horse's lunge threw him back hard against the cantle. The bay was nearly out of sight, swinging off around the trees now, running into the pass as the herd broke away from him.

The red horse caught the excitement, straining his cold-stiffened muscles to keep the pace. Gradually, Sherill was gaining. A high rock mass rushed past and at a narrows he was suddenly in among the racing animals, the bay barely in sight ahead. He caught a brief glimpse of Donovan hanging on the off side of the horse.

He raised the Colt's and took a deliberate

aim and an instant later saw the bay bob into his sights. He squeezed the trigger and breathed the acrid smell of powder-smoke, so intent on his target that he didn't hear the explosion.

A horse ahead of the bay lost his footing and cartwheeled down and two other animals piled into the down one and fell and the ones behind, the bay among them, swung sharply aside and kept going.

The snow blinded Sherill. He wiped his face with his rein hand. Then he rammed the spurs into the sorrel's flanks again. Now the big horse really ran, reaching fast and hard for wind. A gun winked redly out of that seething mass of running animals and a horse alongside Sherill broke stride and fell back. The next instant Sherill saw Donovan sitting erect in the saddle, half-turned, his gun-arm raised.

He was no more than fifty yards ahead and Sherill pulled the sorrel's head sharply to one side and as he swung hard against an animal to his left Donovan's .45 exploded once more.

Sherill didn't know where that second bullet had gone. But now he lined the Colt's and thumbed three swift shots at Donovan's weaving shape. Even before his finger closed on the trigger that last time he was seeing

271

his bullets pounding the man's huge bulk forward in the saddle.

Donovan swayed, fell against the bay's neck and, the bay still running hard, tried to hang on. Then the bay slowed and the sorrel gained on him and suddenly Sherill saw Donovan lose his hold and fall.

The Major's hoarse bellow sounded over the thunder of the hooves and Sherill reined clear of the jam and pulled in. He sat watching the herd pound on past. Then the last few animals ran by and he looked back there to see a red stain against the hoof-churned snow. His glance moved quickly away from it. And now the sorrel's quick and labored breathing was the only sound breaking across the stillness.

He made a wide circle around the spot where Caleb Donovan lay, not looking back. He passed a down animal, making sure the horse was dead before going on. He heard the hollow blast of a shot close ahead and shortly saw a shape move down out of the trees along the slope to his right. It was Jake Henry. Up there, another animal lay in the snow.

The wolfer reined in alongside, not speaking as he saw the look on Sherill's face. They had gone on another hundred yards before Sherill asked tonelessly, "How does it add up, Jake?"

"It adds to two horses and one man, accordin' to my count. I had a chance at another. But he looked like a kid, so I let him go."

Sherill nodded, saying, "Donovan's back there."

"Then that makes it two and two," Jake stated matter-of-factly.

They found Mitch waiting by the trees at the canyon mouth. He looked at Sherill, then at Jake as they rode in on him. He said, "So that winds it up."

They walked their horses across to the fire and threw fresh wood on it and put on some coffee. Shortly, Mitch said, "Jim, I'm goin' up and get Phil. The first thing he'll ask me is if Donovan got away. And, if he didn't, how bad it hurt him to cash in. Should I make up a story?"

"Tell him it wasn't too easy for the Major."

"That's nice," Mitch said, turning away. "Now Phil won't be so sore at missin' this."

Much later, warmed by the fire and the coffee, they headed north out of the pass. The snow was thinning and they could pick out the animals of the herd below, well scattered and aimlessly wandering along a flat and into the timber beyond.

They got to work and by the middle of

the afternoon they made a count of fifty-four. "Close enough," Sherill told Mitch and Phil as they brought in the last gather.

That afternoon Horse first missed Slim in the timber ten miles above the meadow. He noticed the cattle off to his left beginning to lag and drift back through the trees and he rode over there. His shoulders were hunched to bring the slicker against the back of his neck and the water funneled down out of the trough of his wide hat. He called Slim's name a few times. He didn't get an answer.

His anger was quite mild in comparison to his worry. Now he was thinking of all the things Slim had been saying three hours ago as they sat at the fire eating their noon meal. Slim hadn't trusted Donovan, first because he was fairly sure that the Major had killed Ed Stedman last night, next because he saw Donovan using them as bait for Sherill in leaving them back here with the cattle.

So now, having been in the saddle most of the past twenty-four hours, Horse contemplated the prospect of having to work all these cattle alone and didn't like it. Had he been able to see a good reason for it he would willingly have gone on. As it was, the reason was fast becoming obscure.

He was sitting there, cold, tired, listening to the soft whisper of the rain when the sound of the guns rolled faintly down to him from far above.

He listened so intently that he held his breath and was sharply annoyed when his horse shook his head and jingled the bit-chain. Then, when the sound had died out, he said dryly, "The hell with it!" and reined his horse around and headed down through the trees.

Two hours later Jim Sherill — alone and on his way down through the hills — found the Anchor herd scattering slowly out of the trees and along a grassy slope. He made his guess on what happened, and, after a slow circle up through the timber, went on.

He rode the ridge above the meadow just short of dusk and spent some minutes looking down on the deserted layout, so tired that he was halfway tempted to go down to the bunkhouse and take his chances on staying the night there. But finally he swung around to the trail and much later made his camp in the ravine where he and Jake had spent night before last.

That wasn't so long ago, he was thinking as he spread his ground-sheet along a dry spot in under the overhang. He hadn't slept since that night, in fact. A lot had happened since, a few things that mattered and many that didn't.

He was being careful tonight and sleep was what he needed most, so he didn't build a fire and ate a cold meal. When he finally lay back and pillowed his head against the saddle, he was wondering how long it would take Jake, Mitch and Phil to work the horses and the cattle on down to the river.

He had the herd now and it looked like he could keep it this time. But the thing those horses had once represented, his future, seemed unimportant now. Yet here he was with his herd representing more money than he knew what to do with. Two nights ago he had lost his only reason for ever wanting money. Now he could think of Ruth and understand how at odds their lives would have been and be thankful that his future no longer included her.

A pleasing anticipation ran through him as he wondered about tomorrow, about seeing Jean. His thoughts of her idled on until suddenly they brought him to the sharp realization that he would soon be leaving this country. He tried not to think beyond that and he was troubled and almost worried as he finally dropped off to sleep.

He was awake at dawn and in the saddle

twenty minutes later. He crossed the swollen river a few minutes short of ten that morning and a mile further on he swung in along the muddy twin ruts of the Whitewater road at a steady jog.

The air was fresh today and smelled of the rain and of the richness of the land, and the long undulating sweep of grass stretching all the way to the horizon ahead was of a deeper emerald than it had been before the storm.

Some time later he saw a twisting line of freight wagons coming toward him along the road and presently he was passing them, lifting a hand as one driver waved. They were pounding along with a ringing of chains, their four and six teams at a trot, and their hollow banging took his attention and he saw that they were empty. There were nine of them closely following each other and long after he had passed them he heard the sound of their going.

Presently the road dipped down across a shallow coulee and, along its bottom, he found still another high-bodied wagon standing motionless. He came in on it and saw the driver squatting alongside its broken rear wheel. As he pulled in on the sorrel, the driver heard him and straightened, lifting a hand for him to stop.

"Goin' on in to town, stranger?" the driver asked.

Sherill nodded.

"Mind doin' me a favor?"

"Anything you say," Sherill answered.

"Would you stop off at Kramer's yard and tell one of the boys that I'm out here with a busted wheel?"

"Be glad to," Sherill said. He nodded on up the road. "Where are all these empties going?"

"There's a boat twenty miles down the river that run aground. They're tryin' to get as much off her as they can before she busts up in the flood."

Sherill's surprise made him almost reluctant to ask, "She wouldn't be the *Queen*, would she?"

"That's her."

Sherill had been holding his breath. Now he slowly let it out, drawling, "I'll give Kramer your message," and he rode on.

This hard luck sort of spread itself around he told himself, thinking about the *Queen* in a strangely detached way. He was faintly surprised at the oddity of his being so disinterested in this accident that would have meant so much to him several days ago.

Presently he was thinking of other things that revolved about his regret at sooner or later having to leave this country. He was honest enough with himself to admit that it was Jean Ruick, not the country, that he would hate leaving. His deep feelings toward this girl left him quite unsurprised. For a while he wondered about using the hill-ranch as a summer range for horses, tying it in with a half-formed decision to ride over to Fort Selby and have a talk with Lieutenant Ramsay about Ned's offer that he take over the remount business.

He was thinking of those possibilities, and of Jean Ruick, all the rest of the way in to Whitewater. He went in along the street, the sorrel kicking up a muddy spray when he hit the puddles, and turned in at Kramer's lot.

Kramer was the man he spoke to in the office. As an afterthought — after giving the message he had promised to deliver, — he gave his name and asked if he might see Ned's office.

The liveryman said quite affably, "So you're Sherill?" He held out his hand. "Guess I'll be seein' a lot of you. Ned's hangout is at the back. He left an envelope on his desk for you." And he led the way on back to the rear room, leaving Sherill at the door.

The room was small, bare except for the desk, a stove and two chairs. Sherill went across to the desk and stood for a moment looking down at the envelope, not reaching for it. Across its face his name was written.

The writing was Ruth's.

Finally he picked it up and pulled out a single sheet covered with Ruth's flowing script. It read:

Jim Dear:

By now you may know that Ned and I were married this morning. I had hoped against hope that something would happen to bring you back to me and that father would be able to forget that dreadful scene that first night.

Then I got to thinking that you would not come back even if you could. Ned was so sweet and tried to console me. But finally father said that he would never allow our marriage regardless of the outcome. Then, with everything gone wrong, Ned proposed.

Darling, perhaps I married Ned because he was so close to you, because in having him I could still have some part of you. I am so confused now I really don't know. But forgive us both and always believe in —
my love,
Ruth.

Sherill crumpled the letter and dropped it

in the stove. Not a word or a phrase in it had prodded him out of a feeling of amusement; and now it struck him that Ruth's letter might well have been written to someone else and that he was reading it as an onlooker.

He was walking back out to the sorrel when he thought of another thing. And when he rode on it was only as far as a wide alley alongside the bank directly below.

He went in the bank and spent five minutes transferring almost his last dollar to George Lovelace's account. The deposit he made covered not only the Commodore's original loan but the profit he would eventually make from Lovelace's share of the original investment in the herd.

When he finally rode the street again, he was feeling better than he had for days, for weeks. The teller in the bank had told him how to find Judge Ledbetter's house and he turned into the last cross street, glancing on down to the *River House* and feeling no trace of regret. Then he forgot all the unpleasantness with the Lovelaces in his eagerness to see Jean.

Judge Ledbetter's white frame house was the last along the street and sat close to the river. It was one of the few houses in town with grass for a yard and as Sherill turned in to the hitching-post under the big cottonwood he saw a girl in a rust-colored dress kneeling at the edge of the flower-plot that ran the length of the broad porch. There was a basket of flowers beside her and she was cutting fresh blossoms.

He knew the dress and, as he was swinging aground, Jean looked back over her shoulder and saw him. She slowly rose, a look of astonishment crossing her face.

She called, "Jim!" and ran out to meet him.

Then she was standing before him, sober and wide-eyed, trying to judge his smile. Slowly her own smile came and her look was all at once one of outright happiness as she breathed, "You must have had luck."

He nodded. "All there was this time, Jean."

She reached out impulsively and put her hand on his arm, pressing it. "I knew it, Jim. Last night I lay awake so long thinking. I knew I'd see you again."

Her face was radiant, quite beautiful. She laughed softly in delight as she took his arm, turning him out along the yard. "Let's walk on out here while you tell me about it. Judy's such a chatterbox. We won't be able to talk once she knows you're here. I've told her so much about you and she's terribly curious."

"What have you told her?" he asked, looking down at her.

She blushed a little, quickly looking away. "Nothing but the silly chatter girls are always making," she said. Then, more gravely, she asked, "Was it bad, Jim?"

He told her, quite simply but leaving nothing out, about yesterday. And when he had finished they walked on for a time in silence, following the wheel ruts that came out from the street's end and curved over to the river bank. When they came to the down-grade where the road fell to the river, they walked on through the tall grass to the top of the bluff.

Finally she said, "I suppose all little girls must grow up. Do you know how ashamed I've been of Caleb Donovan, Jim? How afraid I was of the truth about him? I was that way until night before last. Then, I suppose, I stopped being a little girl, stopped thinking that my flesh and blood could do no wrong."

"This might not have happened if it hadn't been for me," he said soberly.

She turned quickly toward him. "Don't say that, Jim. Caleb Donovan was an evil man. If it hadn't been for you, a lot more might have happened."

"We'll never know," he said. Then he asked, "What about Brick?"

"We buried him yesterday morning," she

answered quietly.

They stood a long moment without speaking. And now an indefinable awkwardness lay between them until he asked, "What will you do now?"

"I haven't dared think about it, Jim. I suppose the thing to do is just to go ahead and run the place the way dad wanted it run."

"Phil will make you a good man."

"I suppose he will."

She gave him a strange look then, one that was wholly grave as she softly said, "Jim, you're not leaving."

He thought at first he wasn't understanding her and as their glances met he was gripped by an emotion that was a blend of tenderness and respect and an affection he knew rose from deeper within him than any he had ever known.

He knew then that he loved this girl, knew, too, that she already sensed it.

He said, "All that time up there I was thinking of that. Of not wanting to leave."

Her eyes were bright with happiness and as he took her in his arms, her face tilting up to him, Jim Sherill knew that here was everything he had ever wanted.

The employees of THORNDIKE PRESS hope you have enjoyed this Large Print book. All our Large Print titles are designed for easy reading, and all our books are made to last. Other Thorndike Large Print books are available at your library, through selected bookstores, or directly from us. For more information about current and upcoming titles, please call or mail your name and address to:

THORNDIKE PRESS
PO Box 159
Thorndike, Maine 04986
800/223-6121
207/948-2962